The White Light

Vampire Cove - The Red Cliffs

To Fran
Welcome Back

R J Truman

Copyright © 2014 RJ Truman

All rights reserved.

ISBN: 1491216433
ISBN-13: 978-1491216439
Front cover illustrated by Yanni Rust courtesy of Pictured Dreams
Editing by Natalie Rust

Dedication

I don't normally do this kind of thing, but what the hell? I would like to dedicate my second book to the following, jelly bean and Pika Mika. You know who you are.

Books by R J Truman

Book one of 'The White Light Chronicles'
Obsidian White – Shades Of Violet

Book two of 'The White Light Chronicles'
Vampire Cove – The Red cliffs

Coming Soon ...
Book three of 'The White Light Chronicles'
Adrianna – Blue like my heart

Contents

	Prologue	Pg 3
1	The beginning of the end?	Pg 6
2	Rewind	Pg 17
3	Friends with benefits	Pg 22
4	Sweet home Georgiana	Pg 27
5	Holiday!	Pg 29
6	Party Planning	Pg 32
7	Vampirecove.com	Pg 35
8	Time boss please	Pg 43
9	Dream a little dream of me	Pg 47
10	Castle Cove B'n'b	Pg 57

11	The Realm Of The Wolf	Pg 64
12	Rescue Me	Pg 87
13	Dancing In the Dark Side	Pg 94
14	Second Chance, No Choice	Pg 99
15	Too Lost In You	Pg 105
16	No Help For The Helpless	Pg 115
17	The Cup Of Eternal Darkness	Pg 124
18	Destination Lost	Pg 132
19	Is Megan's Times Up?	Pg 136
20	Friends Reunited	Pg 147
21	Fantasies and Fairytails	Pg 149
22	The Blood Red Cliffs	Pg 157
23	Welcome To The Gates Of Hell	Pg 160

PROLOGUE

One Night On Earth

It's a hard life in the Under World even for a vampire, especially a powerful one. Not to mention the most powerful one. Okay so he had everything a man could wish for, a beautiful wife, wealth and a charming enough daughter; however we are not talking about a normal man here. (Not that any man is what I would consider normal.) Although he had all of these things and more, he quickly grew incredibly tired of them, and wanted more. So much more. His wife bored him, as far as he was concerned she was self-obsessed but lacked anything that he would consider to be even close to ambition. He often thought to himself, *what's the point of having wealth if you can never spend it? As you never need to. What's the point in feasting on human souls, if you're never satisfied by them?* And when your daughter talks of humans with flesh and bone and blood that you could feast on, how could you not want that?

He had all the notoriety the Under World could give him, so much so he didn't even need a name! You only had to talk of his appearance, or of the things he did or were about to do and you would know who he was. However, he wanted more, as I said before, much more. He had big aspirations and dreamed of all the things he could do if he roamed free on Earth. All he had to do was to convince Lucifer to set him free. A simple enough task, as far as he was concerned. Lucifer would do anything he wanted, and I do mean anything!

Just one night was all he wanted, or so he said to his master, his creator. After all if his daughter could have a whole lifetime on Earth to walk around, and live as a human. What's one night on Earth for a vampire? What harm could he do? I mean it seemed reasonable enough to the Devil himself. I mean the vampire was only really created to torture human souls and feast on them for eternity in the Under World. He couldn't actually hurt a real human right? These were just some of the seemingly downright lame, and well, totally pathetic justifications Lucifer used to decide that setting his most prized creation free for a night was a good idea. If the 'Almighty One' could let a creature from the deepest pits of the Under World free to live a lifetime on Earth, why not let one out too? After all it was just one night. That's what Lucifer kept telling himself anyway.

Admittedly though, when the Almighty One let Adrianna free, he placed certain limitations on her. However that's a story for another time. Not such strong limitations were put in place when the most powerful of the Under World's vampires was set free. However, plans to stop the vampire from escaping were put in place by Lucifer. That was way before the vampire actually stepped through the Mouth of Hell and onto Earth, thus creating the 'Red Cliffs' that made Vampire Cove, the Gateway to the Under World. That's not me being over dramatic either. Not even a little.

The Beginnings Of An End?

When Hannah Met Richard

Jennifer, Hannah, Amy and Megan had been friends since first school. They were so in sync with each other that even their periods were at the same time. They did everything together, and they were totally and utterly inseparable. Well, that was the case right up until Hannah met Richard, then they weren't so much separated as torn apart. Richard was the one that was doing most, if not all, of the tearing, and Hannah, for a while at least, didn't seem to have the strength or willpower to stop him. She was momentarily weakened by 'love' or Richard's warped manifestation of it.

There were certain stipulations that seemed to suddenly pop into place when Richard entered the scene, these included the following:-

Hannah couldn't go to the cinema with the girls because Richard wouldn't like the film. Regardless of whether he was going or not, if he didn't approve, she wouldn't/ couldn't go.

Richard was vegetarian, so Hannah couldn't go to BBQs as it wouldn't be fair on Richard. Even if vegetarian food was served it was still in the presence of poor dead creatures, killed for the pleasures of dining disgustingly on their flesh. It might seem over the top, but he was very passionate about the mistreatment and eating of animals.

On a lighter note Richard didn't like sand, so Hannah couldn't go to the beach. She might come back with sand in her shoes and get grains in his expensive carpet.

Oh, and here's another one. Richard didn't drink, and well, you get the picture. Plus I'm bored of that game now.

So when the 'happy couple' moved in together, the girls were in turmoil. How could they stop Hannah from making undoubtedly what would be to date the biggest mistake of her life? Hmmmmm, well in short they couldn't. When Hannah had her mind set on something, nothing could make her change it; she was never in the wrong, her decisions were always right. If you didn't agree, well that really was your problem not hers. Guess we can all think of people we know who are like that.

Anyway, back to the, shall we call them, 'happy couple'. As you could probably imagine, their house warming party was so far beyond warm it made the Arctic look like the new Hawaii and, that aside, it was positively dull, for want of a better word. The rules were, (yes there were rules) and I'll keep it brief, no food or any kind of drink to be consumed in the living room. No smoking in any area, inside or out. No shoes beyond the front door. No loud music. No loud talking! I kid you not, I could go on but won't. So as you can imagine, Jennifer, Amy and Megan made their excuses and left early to go to the pub. They couldn't stick to the rules even if they tried, and Richard's attempts at the evil eye were only funny for so long. Hannah surprisingly enough didn't mind though, it meant she got to spend more time alone with Richard. She was nothing if not determined, up to that point anyway, to make the relationship work. She wouldn't fail, she didn't know how.

Richard was incredibly delighted that all her undesirable, and, in his mind, downright vile friends had left. He was even more delighted when everyone else promptly left as well. By 9:00pm the house was deserted, apart from him and Hannah of course. Richard was even more thrilled when Hannah immediately sprung into tidying mode, playing the part of dutiful future house wife. Not wanting to disturb her while she was in full flow, Richard waited until Hannah had washed up and generally cleaned up all the 'mess' from the party, (not that anyone dared to make a mess) before he announced to her. "I'm taking us to the Lake District. You, me, a cottage and some beautiful scenery, what could be better?" He paused, impatiently waiting for her response, once more using his not so evil eyes.

After realising that she had been quiet for far too long she scraped together a reply of sorts.

"Um yeah sounds, lovely?" She couldn't do it, she couldn't lie convincingly any more. Her heart just wasn't in it. Besides, this wasn't a time for missed opportunities, this was a time for action. She longed so much for her old life, for having fun with her friends. She missed all the impromptu trips to places like Ibiza, and Prague. She really yearned for another one of their Saturday night, into Sunday morning drinking sessions. She knew what she wanted, and it wasn't a weekend away with Richard, it was a lifetime away, with the girls. Away from all this. She had tried, she really had. But she knew if she really loved someone, she could be herself. She wouldn't have to try so hard to be something she really wasn't. If they really loved her, then they would love her for who she was, not force her to be something she wasn't, someone was never cut out to be. Who was she attempting to fool? When really, deep down, she knew she wasn't fooling anyone. Hannah had convinced herself that was true, it wasn't selfish to want to be loved. It was selfish of him to want to change her.

The room went silent while Hannah tried to pull together the courage and, more importantly, the right words to ask Richard for a weekend away with her friends. *No, fuck it*, she thought. The old Hannah wouldn't ask for permission to do anything, least of all from a man! Especially a man that right now she didn't even particularly like, or want to be around. Although she had convinced herself this was the right thing to do, she felt scared. She knew that if she did this, and ended it all there would be no going back, no second chances. Richard would never forgive her. But then again she didn't want his forgiveness, not really, she wanted out, she wanted to end it with Richard. She felt confused and needed to clear her head. But there was no time for that.

She took a deep breath, calmed her nerves then decided to take the plunge. "Yeah, so the weekend after the Lake thingy, I'm gonna ask the girls if they wanna go away for a few nights somewhere fun" There it was, the truth. She longed for something fun. She knew Mr. Anti-fun would have something to say about this. But all she could think was bring it on. She and Richard never argued, they never had the passion too. There was no sparks, no fireworks of emotion. Come to think of it, up until now Hannah never saw Richard display any form of emotion towards her at all. That was all about to change.

His voice boomed out full of disapproving rage. "YOU WHAT!?! A weekend away with those drunken whores, with no morals. Did you hear them!? Talking about sex, loudly! In a room full of polite people that didn't want to hear it!"

This was it, the moment she had waited so long for, it was time for them to both show their true colours. "Those 'whores' happen to be my friends. Just because your friends don't have sex, and wouldn't know a blowjob if it came out the toilet and sucked them off, doesn't mean my friends can't talk about it" Hannah hated people disrespecting her closest friends, to her they were her family, and she was fiercely protective of them.

Richard felt like he was seeing red, he hit the wall out of frustration, then turned to face Hannah. "In front of the boss though, Hannah, that is not appropriate behaviour. I will not stand for it in my house, or in my life, and I will not have you spending time with those vile people." There, he said it, her friends were vile. He looked close to being sick when he spat out the words. Little did he know that the boss was more than aware of what the girls were really like, that wasn't really the issue though.

Turned out Richard wasn't the only one seeing red, Hannah could feel her blood boiling.

"Well fuck you then, you lame prick!" She said it. She couldn't take it back. She didn't want to. Besides it was true, he was lame in the prick department. However, he was keen to show he was not so lame in the wrist department. He slapped Hannah hard across the face, and proceeded to ask her to apologise for what she said!

That was it. That was the hard hit of reality that Hannah needed. When she pushed him that's what she got. Anger, and the one thing she would never stand from a man, or from anyone was violence. Hannah left that night, well that second really. She grabbed her phone and left everything else behind. Not that she felt any of it was her's anyway. Not the real her. She expected him to disapprove, she hoped for an argument that would cause him to throw her out. But the stinging pain on her cheek was better than all that. It was a real reason to leave, and one that no one would or could question. Even though she felt hurt, shocked and more than a little scared, she felt like she had won. It had ended, she had got the outcome she wanted. She tried to tell herself that anyway.

On the corner of the avenue where she and Richard had attempted to play happy families, she gave up her façade and fell to the ground convulsing in tears. The true extent of what just happened really hit home. Richard had hurt her. If she stayed, she shuddered, what else would he have done to her. While sitting on the curb she tried hard to compose herself. This wasn't her. She didn't cry, she wasn't weak. She was better than this. She wasn't some silly bint that sat on street corners crying over men, or failed love. She was Hannah. Pep talk over, she swallowed what was left of her ragged pride and dialled up the one person she knew would be there for her.

Megan's phone was ringing like crazy, and to go with that she was dancing like crazy. So in her defence, she could be forgiven for the fact that it took her a little while to notice her phone. Well, in truth it was Jennifer that noticed. "Dude, your fucking bag keeps lighting up like a freaking beacon. If that's Brad, or John or dial-a-dick tell them to piss the hell off. You're not fucking tonight as your out with the ladies." She drunkenly shouted out.

With that Megan finally looked at her phone "Ah well I never, its H to the n to the ahh, ha ha I spelt it wrong oops. I wonder what she wants." She put on her best mock posh voice. "Oh darlings thank you ever so much for coming, one had the most splendid time." Megan and Jennifer fell around in drunken fits of laughter.

Amy jumped up and down, while waving her hands around "AN-SWER IT!" Was her over excited addition to their drunken rambling. She was the only one to realise that the phone was actually still ringing.

Megan laughed even more at her stupidity, she could just about focus on the part of the screen that said accept call. She began tapping at the screen lightly with fingers whose actions were betrayed by alcohol, after several attempts she finally hit the right spot.

Not one to mince her words, Hannah got straight to the point. "He hit me, then I left" Was not the opening line to the conversation that Megan expected to hear. In all the years she had been friends with Hannah, it was one of the few things she never ever thought she would hear. It was right up there with, "I'm going lesbian". Hannah didn't take shit from men. For all his faults, Megan didn't think even Richard could turn out to be this shit.

Holding the phone a bit too close to her mouth she shouted out "I'll fucking kill him! The bastard! No one beats up one of my girls and lives". Megan sounded like an angry Madame from a whore house, but she spoke the truth, she really did for that brief second want to kill him.

Confused with how the conversation was going "What? What? What?" The others crowed in unison.

Megan turned to the girls, and in her best attempt to sound official, said "Ladies, fuck this shit hole, we are on a mission to save Hannah." Then, remembering she was still on the line, asked, "Han, where are you?"

Hannah tried desperately to string a few more words together "On the corner of my road" was all she managed to get out before crying again!

Rewind

To fully understand the story of how Hannah and Richard met you need to go back to the start. Richard was a spoilt little rich boy, who in order to inherit his families wealth was told he needed to get a job, and make his own way in the world. It didn't stop him from being flash with the cash, or should I say credit card, though. He couldn't bear the thought of not having the best of everything. After all it was how he was raised. He also hated the idea that his family cut off his allowance. How dare they? How could they throw him out into the big bad world and be so sure that they would watch him fail? But he was going to show them they were wrong, show everyone that they were wrong, that he could make it on his own. So he got a job in an office with the view to working his way up, and one day becoming a manager.

When Hannah found out the new guy in the office, (aptly nick named Big Dick, by her friends, and for obvious reasons) was loaded in more ways than one, (he wore very tight incredibly expensive trousers,) well, like a lot of women would, she just had to get her teeth into him. As I've already mentioned what Hannah wanted, Hannah got.

Richard was so very unlike Hannah, as we have already discussed. He was dull, boring, and lacked in any hint of anything remotely resembling a personality. Due to this, Megan, Amy and Jenn couldn't imagine that he was any good in bed, and then soon re-named him 'The Useless Big Dick'. He was useless in the office where they all worked, but despite this the other ladies all still loved him. Well, they loved to look at him. He worked out and was very easy on the eye. Due to a diet of vegetarianism and no alcohol, there was not an ounce of anything on him that could have been mistaken for fat. And thanks to the fact he wore, as I said before, ridiculously, almost inappropriately tight trousers. Leaving very little to even the blandest, or most innocent imagination. This was all part of his plan to lure in the ladies. Give them a hint of what he had to offer. And also to hide the fact that he had no real skills or talents.

Based on his money and looks alone it was easy to see how Hannah, shallow as she was, could fancy him. But what did he see in her? Hannah was a bed hopping party girl, always turning up late for work in the clothes she wore on the night before the night before. She got away with this as she was good at her job when she was there, and the bosses loved her, in shall we just say, more ways than one. Richard loved the looked of her too, in her shorter than scandalous skirts she was very eye catching. Even this strict vegetarian couldn't deny that he had a need for that piece of meat. Plus she was easy, and therefore an easy target. She liked pretty shiny things, so all he had to do was give her a taste of the highlife, and she would fall at his feet. How wrong could he be?

To look at they were a hot couple. Although after a few months of dating him Hannah soon went from hot to damp, to stone cold sober. Everyone could see that he was killing her. Slowly draining everything out of her that made her so alive. So what if they had the house, the car, the cat, dog, and the fish? Well, maybe not the cat and the dog. Richard had 'allergies'. However they didn't seem to have any passion or fun. Hannah, despite all that, seemed happy enough on the surface. Inside she was screaming out for wild nights, great sex and partying. Inside, Richard was as placid as he was outside. In his head he had tamed a party girl, sculpting her into his ideal wife. Ready for his ideal wedding, and getting all his money. That was all he really wanted, his families money. You wouldn't believe he would care so much about it. But he did, even more than he cared about animal rights, or having a trophy wife. He wanted people to envy him because he was better than them. Better, he thought, than anyone.

The second Hannah mentioned wanting to go out partying, something deep inside him stirred. How could she still want that? Want them? And now, after he had planned out the whole engagement weekend in the Lake District, it was too much. He flipped. There was emotion lurking under his placid exterior, violent emotion. The only kind Hannah wasn't expecting to find, the kind which had her fleeing to the safety of her friends. Friends he thought she was better than. Friends that she'd had since first school. Friends she had relied on to get her through life. Hannah would never say she used people, she just collected friends that were, shall we say, beneficial to her.

As for her family, they never really had time for her. They were all about her brother. He was amazing at everything he did. He was a straight A, straight laced kind of guy. Never got into trouble, never went out. Even though he had friends, they were happy to stay in and do 'safe' things like play chess. Or had homework clubs. He was all the things Hannah wasn't, so she developed a very different approach to getting noticed. Needless to say her parents didn't approve of her behaviour, but it got their attention regardless of whether they approved or not. It didn't take long, however, before she grew tired of vying for their love, and turned her attention instead to a more worthy cause, to her friends. Making them her family.

Friends With Benefits

I think that now it's time I gave you a proper introduction to Hannah's friends, give you a little insight into why Hannah handpicked these select few to be her lifelong 'girlfriends.' To become what would be her substitute family. You'll find out some more about the girls and their friendship with Hannah as you read their parts in this story. Of course, if Hannah got her way, it would be all about her. It was always all about her. Apart from where her family were concerned. And so for Hannah's sake I'll keep this bit brief.

Let's start with Megan, Hannah's best friend. Megan was incredibly intelligent, but instead of using her brain she alternately got by on her cute and innocent looks at school. She was quiet and hardworking to a point. However, if on the rare occasion she forgot to do her homework she always got away with it. After all it was very unlike her to purposely not do her homework. Even if she was out playing, or later partying with friends she still found time to fit in a little learning. In the classroom her quiet and demur persona always won the teachers over. Not to mention her huge brown eyes, and long ever fluttering lashes.

Hannah quickly noticed that Megan was a big hit with the teachers, and so would always try and sit next to Megan in class. This was so she would be associated as being friends with the 'good girl.' Also it was so she could copy her notes, and her answers in tests. Megan was always one of the top scorers in class tests. It's because of Megan that Hannah got through school. Megan wrote practically most, if not all, of Hannah's coursework, and Hannah often had fun convincing the teachers, (thankfully for Hannah they were mostly male) that the work was all hers. When Megan got her job at the offices of Hampton and Hampley's, she introduced Hannah to the boss. Knowing that Hannah would use her own skills, and female persuasion to secure herself a job.

It's hard to see what Megan got out of the 'friendship'. Well, I guess she got a friend. Being cute and quiet, she was also timid, and not very outgoing. So when a pretty blonde girl wanted to sit next to her, and talk to her she wasn't going to say no. So what if she only wanted to copy her notes. It was still better than not having any friends at all.

Hannah made friends with Jennifer at the same time as she made friends with Megan. Jennifer was that angry red haired girl that liked to tease the boys. Even at a young age with her deadly combination of red hair, green eyes and pure pale skin, she was just like Christmas. Hannah realised over the years that males were attracted to Jennifer, but quickly got scared off by her temperamental mood swings. So as soon as Jennifer picked them up, Hannah was there to win them over. With her natural blonde hair and blue eyes, and seemingly placid temperament, Hannah seemed like a good alternative to the human firework that was Jennifer.

Jennifer, like Megan and Hannah, had also gotten a job at Hampton and Hampley's. She secured herself the position as a PA, she didn't take any messing from anyone, and was great at organising things from car hire to works parties. No one dared say no to Jennifer, they wouldn't risk facing her wrath.

Why was Jennifer friends with Hannah? Simple. Girls didn't like Jennifer. She was mean, and didn't take shit from anyone. When

Hannah came on the scene and didn't seem to mind her meanness, Jennifer saw no reason to not be friends with her. She liked Hannah's 'I'm the best' screw you attitude. So they gelled straight away.

Finally we come to Amy, Hannah made friends with Amy to make herself look more intelligent. In truth, Amy had more brains than Hannah, she just didn't always apply them correctly. She had a short attention span, and would often drift off in to daydreams in the classroom. When a teacher would ask her a question she would often come out with a random response, if anything at all; which quickly gave her the reputation as being your classic ditsy dumb and not quite so natural blond. Although when it came to exams Amy would often get as high a mark, sometimes higher, than Megan, she would just play dumb to fit her place in the group.

She also worked in the office along with the other girls. They found that all the way through life they functioned better as a team. Unlike the others, with their high-flying roles, Amy worked as a receptionist. She was bubbly and friendly, and with her warm personality she was good at welcoming existing and potential clients to the company.

Come the weekend, all the girls liked to party. From their early teens onwards they would drink, get drunk, and have fun with the boys. All using their own merits to win them over. During the week Megan would remain professional. Jennifer would try her best to save her energy for the weekend, when she could let out some of her built up anger from the week. Amy would continue to dumb down, so as not to threaten people with her words of wisdom and hidden intelligence. Hannah, on the other hand, would carry on being Hannah, regardless of what day it was. That was until she met Richard, and well, we know what happened to her then.

Sweet Home Georgiana

As you've probably heard me mention a few times, the girls all loved to party. Most of their crazy drunken antics took place in their home city. The beautiful city of Georgiana. Name sound familiar? Well it should. It's where Obsidian and Rowena moved to when they left the magical forest.

Any way enough about them, let's find out a little bit more about the city itself. As I've told you before the city was built in Georgian times. But its history spans way back before that. To a time when invading shit was all the rage. In a way it still is. However back then it was all swords and hot men in little leather skirts fighting like real men.

I kid you not.

The city is built on the site of an extinct volcano. Volcanoes are a direct link to the Under World. Which probably explains why the vampire that escaped the Under World was attracted to the place.

All the warmth and power left in the stones and soil reminded him of home.

As for the city nowadays, it's a labyrinth of shops, bars, and underground clubs. Great for vampires and humans alike to party and play side by side. So it's not hard to see why the girls had so much fun there.

Holiday!

Now, back to those ill-fated party girls in question. In full flow now, she couldn't contain herself. "Well he was just a Big Dick! Basically A big floppy dick, both his heads were useless, pretty but fucking useless!" Hannah giggled.

Hannah was back. In the back of the taxi, with her best friends around her, she had finally come back to life. She had never felt so alive. So ready to take on anything. This was the start of something, and she was hoping deep down it was something good.

After the girls had rescued her from the street corner she was sobbing on, they bundled her in to the back of a taxi, and then listened half-heartedly to her moaning all the way back to Megan's house. When they got there she finally stopped whining and started smiling. She said was done with men, well, Richard that was for sure. She announced to the girls that she was eager and ready for anything. Well, I say that now. I don't think anyone could seriously be ready for what was coming to them. I know I, for one, wouldn't be.

So while she still had what she thought was their full attention, she also brought up the idea for the weekend away. Well, she didn't have any time to lose, now was the time for action. Or so she kept telling herself. So far it had definitely been a night full of action.

Using up the last of her energy "I think we should get this weekend booked now!" Were Amy's last words before she passed out on Megan's sofa.

Jennifer put a throw over her to keep her warm, and reached out for Megan's laptop. Megan jumped up and blocked Jennifer's way, "Um, what you doing?" Megan was always fiercely protective of her laptop. She was a keen writer but would never let anyone read her stuff. Well, apart from the teachers who marked her GCSE and A level coursework. It was one of the few times she got straight A's based on her actual intellectual abilities alone. Well, almost.

Jennifer shrugged her shoulders "OK, well I was just gonna hook up the net and have a browse, find a little get away for us ladies, but hey ho, I won't bother. I mean I wasn't gonna read one of your precious stories, might delete one though for all the good they do on there. I mean it's not like we get to read them!" Jennifer's fiery drunken temperament had finally awoken. She flicked back her long red hair. She was a natural red head, but liked to vamp it up with red low-lights. When she was angry they seemed to intensify in colour, like she really was red hot and ready to explode.

The tension between the girls was growing, and it was more than Hannah could bear. She had seen enough fighting first hand that evening, and couldn't take any more "Now, now. I think I've seen enough heightened emotions for one night. Jenn, go home, go to bed, and don't call any one." Hannah winked at Jennifer, who smiled a suggestive smile back. They both knew exactly what Jenn needed in order to release her pent up, ummm, anger shall we say?

Party Planning

Lucifer had all the plans in place for the release of his most feared and precious creature. He both loved (if you could call it that), and envied the vampire. For he was more feared in the Under World than Lucifer himself. Lucifer had decided what would happen, and a fool proof plan was laid out. Or so he thought. The plan was thus: One night in the Vampire Castle on Earth. The castle would be transported up to Earth, and the vampire would be confined to it. One night, that's how long he was allowed. He couldn't risk any longer for he feared the wrath of the Almighty. What would he do to Lucifer if he discovered he had let a creature from the deep roam around, not exactly free on Earth? Take the Under World from him? Take his power? He shuddered. He was feeling very uneasy all of a sudden. Was the Almighty One already aware of his plan? He couldn't think of that now, he had to set the plan in motion.

As for what the vampire would do on Earth to amuse himself that was simple enough. Feast on the blood and flesh of real humans. Not just off of their hollow, dry, cold, bitter souls, but their living, breathing, warm, and blood filled flesh. Lucifer had already carefully selected the vampire's victims. A group of girls looking for a 'good time' at the weekend. But these were no ordinary girls, they were marked. Marked for him. For Lucifer to claim as his own. After a brief 'Goth' phase they went through in their early teens, and a few somewhat faked suicide attempts in a sad bid to get attention, they had in fact caught someone's attention. Maybe not the attention they were hoping for though. Lucifer got to decide whether or not he wanted the souls for his own. He had decided the mark was upon them. Not a mark you or I could see. It was a mark on their souls. He made the decision to watch them, and to follow their actions. A decision that seemed now to work in his favour. He could dispose of the girls, and treat his prize creation at the same time. Little did Lucifer know though that the vampire he was going to release was making plans of his own. Big plans.

***

Hannah tried hard to sleep but her head was filled with darkness, and despair. Screams from disembodied voices rang in her ears.

Eyes burned brightly into her mind, watching her from the inside, reading her thoughts. Whilst planting thoughts of their own. A swarm of black birds shifted in and out of focus. Always there, always present. They were the darkness, and among them were the souls, ever desperately trying to make a bid for freedom.

"I'm coming for your soul" was twisting around the screams. Everything went black, like the birds had become one giant mass of shadows, and the screams drifted around like grey mist.

"'I'm coming for your soul" dripped down the walls of her mind as red as blood. She woke up in a cold sweat. Far away Lucifer was laughing. Oh how he loved mind games. She blinked. Black eyes this time. She saw dark, midnight black eyes. But she was awake, wasn't she? Far away Lucifer was in fits of laughter. Oh she is so easy to mess with. Easy, but fun.

www.vampirecove.com

The next day Hannah decided to hijack Megan's laptop and look up holiday locations. She was ready to face Megan's wrath, after all, she had a very good reason for using it. Hannah tried hard to block out the vivid dreams of screams and torment from the night before. It was just a dream. Maybe a reflection on the fear she was now feeling towards Richard. How would he react to her new freedom? Would he come back for her? That's what it was about. Well that's what she tried to tell herself. It was little comfort to her now though. The images were playing over and over in her mind, and try as she might, she just couldn't shift them. The screams, and those tiny black birds that guarded them, it was still filling her head. There was something else in that darkness, a shape, a figure, maybe more than one. Twisted and mangled together. She blinked hard, as she thought she could stop the black and distorted figures creeping out of her mind. It was like they were dancing around in Megan's front room.

Trying not to get distracted by things she knew weren't really there, (or so she told herself) she forced herself to concentrate even more on what she was attempting to do. "They're not real," she said, tearing her eyes away from the wall. She stared blankly at the monitor, trying to focus on the job at hand wasn't easy. Not when her mind was so clouded up. Full of big ominous storm clouds of fear and emotions. She had to get away, to find a place to escape to. She told herself she needed to get away from all the drama, it was clearly getting to her. She was seeing things. She needed a place where she and the girls could have fun, and have a well deserved catch up. Where they could all be themselves again, like when they were much younger. Before men took over them, and their lives. One place kept popping up again and again. Hannah kept deleting the pop up, but after a while she gave up and clicked on it.

"Welcome to VAMPIRE COVE. Aptly named due to the shape of the ancient cave, blah blah blah, boring" Hannah was about to click on the X to clear the page when something stopped her. A voice in her head and a flash on the screen of those eyes. Those coal black eyes. They sparkled then faded. A chill ran over her body, she shivered, part with fear, part with pleasure. Something told her that those soulless eyes needed her. Needed her soul. Those eyes had burned their way into her memories, and try as she might, she just couldn't shift them. It was like they were a part of her now, watching her every move, like a pair of extra eyes hidden deep inside her. She remembered the eyes in her dream. And tried hard to push the Image away. Something in the room made her jump almost literally out of her skin. It's OK she told herself, it's just Megan. "Hey Meg, don't be mad OK? Sorry I'm using your laptop. But I've booked our weekend away." Megan had just appeared round the corner of her living room door. She was still in her night clothes, a slinky nightdress, and PJ bottoms, teamed with fluffy slippers and a thick, warm looking dressing gown. Her face lit up with a beaming smile, she looked so excited.

Almost jumping up and down with joy, Megan finally managed to get some words out "Oh my god don't tell me, Paris, no no wait, Rome. Oh no still too romantic, Ibiza. Ummm oh wait huhhh Vegas. LA?" She really was jumping up and down now by this point. She, for once, couldn't care less who was using her precious laptop, she was going on holiday!

Hannah glanced up at Megan, then back down at the laptop. "Er no, I thought we could all use a little detoxing, relaxing fun. I've booked us in at a health spa" Hannah said sounding almost apologetic.

"A What!" Megan's face dropped. She shook her head and walked out the room.

Hannah shut the laptop and shouted after Megan "What, it will be fun" Hannah thought it could be fun anyway. She was sure they could make it fun. There was a time when they could make an thing exciting.

Megan made an emergency group phone call to Jennifer, and Amy. At some point in the night Amy had woken up and decided she needed her own bed. It wasn't her usual walk of shame home, but she still felt every bit as terrible as she normally would, her hangover was killing her.

With all the girls on the line Megan announced "Hey girls, we have a problem" There was no mistaking the worry in Megan's voice. Amy stretched and glanced at her phone "Hmmm" was her response. She was still half asleep and hadn't realised she had accepted the call.

"Ahhhhhummmm!" a rather loud sigh/yawn was Jennifer's. She too was only half with it.

Megan glared angrily at her phone, it wasn't going to be easy to get any sense out of the girls but she wasn't giving up. "You know we thought we had her back?" She sat back down in her chair and waited for some type of coherent response.

Both the girls were still clearly very confused "Who" they replied in unison.

Megan rolled her eyes and hit her hand down on the arm of her chair "Hannah!" She shouted back, rather annoyed down the phone.

Both the girls were slowly waking up "Oh," and "yeah right" followed. They tried hard to care. However their hangovers were numbing their abilities to truly express their real feelings. The only things they felt were pain and maybe a little nausea.

Megan could sense she was losing her already less than interested audience, so cut straight to the point. "Anyways so she has booked us in at a health spa!"

Amy sat up in bed "Fuck, really?" She suddenly sounded more awake.

"Hell no, really?" was Jennifer's reply.

Hannah spent the rest of the day trying to convince the girls that it's just what they needed. Really cleansing for the soul, was how she tried to sell it. However the girls remained unconvinced. They text and plotted ways to get Hannah to change her mind. They had ideas from booking another weekend away, but that would be way too expensive, to making Hannah go on her own, after all she was the one who's soul needed cleansing. Too harsh. To locking Hannah in a room till she came to her senses. Too simple. After a while the girls thought they would call it a day, and continue the plotting over emails. Much cheaper than using all their text messages. Although had any of them bothered to check their contracts they would have realised the texts were free! Intelligence and common sense don't always come hand in hand.

The next day the office was buzzing with talk about how Hannah had cheated on Richard, Richard was gay, Hannah's too much of a slut to settle down, etc., etc. All the gossip stopped however when Hannah arrived, black eye, and bruised face on full display.

Megan had begged her to try and cover it up. But no, Hannah wanted the world, well, the office at least, to see how much of an evil woman beater Richard really was. After all it was the integral part of her plan. The one that involved her proving to everyone it wasn't her fault. Needless to say Richard didn't show up. He sent in an email with a lame excuse as to why he would no longer be coming into the office. It was clear from his email that he really wasn't cut out for a role in magazine publishing.

When Megan, Amy, and Jennifer all logged into their emails, aside from the work related stuff they deleted, and the emails from the office gossips desperate to know what really went down between Richard and Hannah, they all had an urgent email sent from Hannah.

When they opened it they all saw the link www.vampirecove.com Intrigued by what exactly Hannah had in store for them they each clicked on the link. When it opened they were treated to a short film.

"Hello ladies. I'm waiting for you to join me in my most splendid castle, in the beautifully named, Vampire Cove. The gateway to all you've ever dreamed and desired. I'll make all your naughty dreams, and fantasies come true. Come party with me, it will be fun!"

The video featured a man half dressed, and showing his very appealing looking chest. He had long midnight black hair, coal dark eyes, and moonlight pale skin. He showed the girls his ballroom, dining room, then finally his bedroom, as he gave his tour of his castle. It was elaborately decorated, lots of gold, lots of rich red and purple fabrics. Marble floors, high ceilings, chandlers, stained glass windows. It looked divine. The last room they were shown was the bedroom, with one large four post bed, thick, warm, cosy blankets... and handcuffs! What more could a girl ask for? In the case of these girls, nothing. They were drawn in and captivated by the idea of the place. Vampire Cove was the place to be. The place they needed to be. They had all forgotten it was meant to be a health spa! But fun was good for your health, right? All they needed now was to get the time off work. Which given their powers of persuasion shouldn't prove too hard a task for any of them.

Time Boss Please

Due to the fact that all four girls worked in different departments, getting time off together wouldn't normally be a problem. This was however a busy time in the office as a new magazine was about to be launched. Hampton and Hampley's specialised in house and home magazines, showing people the kind of houses most of us could only dream about. Launch time was always mega hectic. So due to this the girls had to really use those powers of persuasion I mentioned earlier. Not that it was actually a problem for any of them.

Well, Amy got off lightly. As the receptionist she simply said that although her job was important, most of the marketing, and events held for the launch were away from the office, so they could get someone else to fill in for her while she was away. With her holiday booked all Amy then had to think about was packing. As it was only a long weekend. Only one suitcase would be needed, or so you would think. Unsure as to what the weather would be like at the coast, Amy packed for all eventualities, including snow! Well, you never know, it could snow in August.

Jennifer had a slightly more difficult time trying to get the days off. So she needed to pull together all of her organisational skills, and sort everything well in advance for her boss. As she was meticulous at arranging everything, she had even arranged back up plans for her backups, just to make sure that everything was taken care of while she was away. She would take her work phone with her. She had it unlocked, and had SIMs from all major networks set up ready to use, just to make sure she could be contacted should anything go wrong. She also arranged a car to be ready to pick her up should she need to return to the office for any reason. She left a list of her phone numbers on her boss's desk, and set a reminder on her phone to contact her boss as soon as she arrived, so her boss would know what number was best to contact her on. Everything was covered, and there was no reason for him to say no to her. There was nothing he could say no to. She didn't need to wear the green low cut dress that perfectly showed off her curves, made her skin look like snow, and her hair look like fire. But wear it she did, and none of the men in the office were complaining. A few women did though.

Megan got to play the best friend card. As Hannah's best friend she had to help out in her hour of need. Plus, as assistant editor to one of the company's other well established magazines, she wouldn't be needed for the launch. Although she would miss all the freebies at the launch party, she knew that her other friends in the office would save some for her. All she had to concentrate on was packing. She was a more sensible packer than Amy, and just packed a few key items. Jeans, a few different tops, cute underwear, and swimwear. She was ready to go in no time.

Hannah, being Hannah, didn't need any excuses. The black eye was enough to get her out of anything. Plus no one really wanted an emotional wreck hanging around the office. Especially one who was looking for ways of getting over her ex. She was once quoted as saying in an article she, um shall we say, 'convinced' someone (I'll name no names) to publish, "The best way to get over a man is, to get under another". It was an article about, well, no one was really sure. Hannah was annoyed with Megan as she had slept with someone Hannah liked, so Hannah got some work published in Megan's magazine just to rub it in her face. Hannah was nice like that. She even got to do a photo shoot in a nice posh county house. In her words 'it helped keep it in theme with the magazine', it was more likely an excuse to show the world how amazingly beautiful she was. That being said there were some references to decorating in the article. But most were plain innuendo.

Dream A Little Dream Of Me

"Oh my god who ordered the limo!" Amy cried out as she peered through Megan's plush gold and red floral handmade living room curtains. It was the day the girls were due to leave for the cove, and they decided to have an all-night drinking session at Megan's place before they left. What better way to start a detox than to be full of alcohol? Made perfect sense really.

"Hm" Hannah flipped back her long blonde ponytail, she often tied her hair up before she went to sleep, and it kept it nice and neat for when she woke up. Sometimes she would sleep with a mirror and make-up under her pillow. So she could whip it out in the morning and make sure she looked extra amazing for whoever she woke up with. That was before she met Richard. She carefully peeled herself off of Megan's cream leather sofa and tried her best to stretch. The few nights she spent without her memory foam mattress were taking their toll on her, especially her back.

She limped over to the window trying to regain the use off her legs, but pins and needles had taken hold of them, and were not giving up without a fight.

Megan came bounding down the stairs, fully dressed and with wet hair. Her brown hair seemed almost black. It was clear she had just got out of the shower. Her vest top was sticking to her wet skin. But that couldn't be the reason she was so excited. "It's done, finished, finally!" She was clearly very happy about something, and it wasn't the weekend away.

"What is?" Hannah asked in an attempt to sound interested. While stomping her feet hard on the floor, in a desperate bid to get her legs to work.

Megan turned her attention to Hannah, and tried hard not at laugh at what her friend was doing. She wasn't going to ask Hannah what she was doing, it wasn't about Hannah right now. "My book! Sex, lies, and school girls, I finished it all last night when you guys finally passed out!" She cried out in excitement.

"Speak for yourself!" Jennifer walked into the living room, looking hanging. Her red hair scraped up into a bun. She was wearing a loose thin hoodie, jogging bottoms and her favourite sheepskin lined suede boots. "What! I tried to get some sleep but all I could hear was the endless tap, tap, tapping of her bloody stupidly loud keyboard" Jenn pointed at Megan, and gave her the best evil eyes she could muster given her lack of sleep.

Trying hard to change the subject back to their break, Amy shrieked out excitedly "Well never mind all that, it's time to go!" As the sun was shining she decided to wear a tiny little summer dress. She had changed while Hannah was asleep.

The only one not dressed, or showered was Hannah. On realising this she announced that they should go ahead and she would meet them in the car in ten, maybe twenty minutes, which would be a much more realistic time frame.

Thankfully she already had her clothes packed. Megan and Jennifer had made a trip round to Hannah and Richard's old place to pick up her stuff. Richard wasn't there but his mother was. She threw Hannah's clothes at them in bin bags from the first floor window. Not very polite of her considering what her son had done. That aside, they collected up the bags and piled them up in Megan's car. Being the nice friends that they were, they also made a trip to a 24 hour supermarket and purchased 4 large pink leopard print suitcases to put Hannah's stuff in. They knew the sight of seeing her expensive designer clothes and accessories in bin bags would tip her over the edge.

After a quick shower, (well quick for her) Hannah threw on jeans and a vest top, grabbed a suitcase and dragged it to the limo. She had every faith in her friends that they would have packed practically for her. Indeed they had. Each case contained a selection of her underwear, jeans, swimwear, going out and casual tops, and short little party dresses. Every eventuality was covered.

Inside the limo the girls had already cracked open a bottle of champagne and were in full drinking flow. Amy reached over and passed a glass to Hannah, but she dismissed it. The combination of loud music, and the insanely bright disco lights that beat and pulsed in time to the music were seriously not helping Hannah's headache. She closed her eyes just for a second. Or so she thought.

She was looking around the interior of the limo when something caught her attention. "Oh look, there's something back here!" She called to the others, but they didn't hear her. She pulled aside a curtain at the back of the limo. It was heavy and made of a lavish velvet like fabric. It felt much softer than velvet though, and despite its weight it had an odd fluidity to it. It was almost more liquid than fabric but unlike liquid it didn't feel wet. She pushed her head through the gap in the curtain. It was almost like she was going through a waterfall. Unsurprisingly, she could even hear the sound of running water.

Gazing though the gap it took her eyes awhile to take in what she was looking at. *They couldn't seriously fit all this in the back of a limo, could they*? She shook her head not believing what she was seeing.

Excited to share what she was seeing she turned her head back to call out to the others. "Guys, they have a pool or something back here!" She shouted out to them. Still no response, it was like they couldn't hear her. Stuff them then, she thought, and decided to go it alone.

As she crawled the rest of the way through the black fluid curtains her hands met the cold feel of marble. She crawled forward a little more and blinked till her eyes fully adjusted. The room was lit by a large black candelabra hanging from the ceiling, and several black candles that were strategically dotted around for ambient effect. The marble looked almost gold in colour, and was smooth under her palms, not slippery like Hannah had expected.

In the centre of the room, sunk into the floor was a large pool or bath. It was filled with a rich dark red coloured liquid. At the far end of the pool was a man. He had the same dark eyes as the one in her dream and that she had seen on the internet. He had midnight dark hair and moonlight pale skin. Hannah could only see him from the waist up, the rest was submerged in the pool. What she could see she liked a lot. It took her back to her younger 'Goth' days, when she was all about men with long, dark hair and a mean moody look in their eyes.

Gesturing a hand to her he broke the silence "Come, join me, it's lovely and warm in here, but a little lonely" He spoke with a tempting smile on his face.

Unsure how to proceed, Hannah decided that standing up was a good place to start. As she did so she fixed her eyes on the pool. "The um pool, what's it filled with?" Hannah asked in a voice that sounded more seductive than her own. She glanced form the pool to his toned stomach, to his eyes, back to the pool.

The smile widened on his lips as he spoke again "Berry juice, of course. Warm, rich, berry juice. Try some, it's good." He paused between each word as he spoke, adding a dramatic edge to his words. As for his actions, he ran his hand through the liquid and let it drip through his fingers. It did look like berry juice. Well, Hannah tried to convince herself that it did.

Hannah was confused. All of a sudden she found herself shamelessly stripping off. Not that it was unlike her to take her clothes off in the presence of a man, but this man was a totally stranger. Or was he? She felt like she had known him forever. It was the eyes, she told herself, defiantly the eyes. One look and they could make her do almost anything. Well they could certainly make her strip off.

Before she had time to really think about what she was doing, she was slinking her way sexily over to the pool. Slowly and seductively she lowered her naked self into the warm, rich red liquid. It was like she had lost all sense of self control. She had never been a strong swimmer, but now she was effortlessly gliding through the warm dark crimson liquid. The pool was deceptively big, and went on and on. After what felt like forever, she was finally facing the man. He fixed his dark black diamond eyes on her deep blue ones, searching for a way through them. To her heart, to her soul. Then, when he had her full attention he reached back down into the liquid, letting it collect on his fingertips. Slowly, he raised his hand out of the pool and dripped some of the red liquid playfully on to his pale, toned chest. As he did so, Hannah couldn't resist any longer, she reached out and touched him, placing her hand on his chest. She was startled for some reason, she wasn't expecting him to feel so warm. No he wasn't warm he was blazing hot.

Sensing her confusion he spoke again "The fires of the other world, burn warm through my veins" He responded to the question that Hannah hadn't even asked, not out loud anyway. Purely to make sure she wasn't imagining it she touched him again, running her hand thoughtfully down his chest

While she was still captivated by him he dripped more of the liquid on himself. "Try some." He spoke softly as he held his hand out to her. Hannah licked the excess liquid off of his fingers. It tasted warm, and metallic, not like berries at all, but more like blood? That wasn't the biggest shock of all, the biggest shock to her was that she liked it. She wanted more, so she cupped her hands and dipped them into the blood. She let the warm rich liquid fill her palms. Slowly and cautiously she raised her hands trying hard not to spill too much of the precious liquid. She lowered her head to her cupped hands, her lips were poised and ready to drink. Just as she was about to sip it down, something stopped her. Like a slap round the face.

Jennifer looked out of the window of the limo, and realised they had arrived, she grabbed Hannah and started shaking her. "Hannah hun, wake up, we are here" Jennifer's voice was full of apprehensive excitement.

Hannah abruptly woke up from what she was sure felt like a few seconds power snooze. "What? Already? That was quick!" Hannah was more than a bit disappointed by the news of their arrival. Her dream was just getting good.

Looking at her like she was crazy, Amy tried hard not to have a full on laughing fit. The champagne was in full flow in her blood stream. But she tried to sound sober "Um OK, well, you've been asleep for the whole journey, which was fine, as it meant more drink for us". It was no good, Amy giggled, letting slip that she was a little more than tipsy. Composing herself she continued, "We were having a catch up about old times, you remember that crazy lady that came to our first school and talked to us about loving trees and stuff? Well Meg was saying she saw her the other day, and she hadn't aged a day! Like, looked totally the same. I mean weird, or what?"

The door to the limo opened as if by itself, cutting Amy's drunken ramble short. The girls didn't see who opened it, come to think of it they didn't even see who was driving the car, although they didn't really care now that they had arrived. After drinking their fill of what seemed to be a never ending bottle of champagne, the girls stumbled one by one rather ungraciously out of the limo.

Castle Cove B'N'B

What met their eyes was not at all what they expected. The lavish looking castle in the emails was nowhere to be seen. Instead, they were faced by a run down, weather beaten red brick building. It had large, all be it broken, windows, with rotten wooden frames, and shutters that flapped in a cold, chilling wind. A welcome sign swung from a rusted bracket above the front door. The door looked like someone had kicked it in, and someone else had made a rather poor effort at repairing it. Tiny little black flies swarmed around the building, shrouding it from on looker's eyes. Not that it was much to look at. In fact it looked like a shit tip. But these weren't flies that were hanging around it. They were something else. Little tiny birds, and where there are tiny birds there is usually trouble.

"Great" Hannah muttered this was just what she needed. A disaster of a mini break. She thought the mystery limo was too good to be true. This was not what she booked, or paid for. Not that she could actually remember having to pay anything when she booked. Now she could see why. No one with any sense would step foot inside the door, but then again the girls weren't always the most sensible of people.

****

Lucifer had tried his hardest to disguise the building. I mean you couldn't just place a beautiful gleaming pure ruby castle on top of some cliffs and hope that no one would notice. It might bring a little unwanted attention to itself. So he settled for the more demure red brick façade. With a touch of dilapidated weather beaten woodwork, he was very pleased with the overall look of the castle once it arrived safely at its destination.

He was also incredibly amused by the girl's reactions. He could have watched their disgusted faces for an age, however he had more important things to do. Like making sure his vampire protégé stuck to the plan. Not that he listened much to Lucifer anyway. Not that Lucifer would never admit it though as he liked to play the proud parent. He would never utter the words "you disappoint me" about his favourite child. How could he, when the vampire had achieved so much? Jealously however, is something you should never underestimate.

***

Amy uncrossed her arms she was not impressed "Well I'm not staying here". Her dress was blowing up in the wind, and she battled with it to try and keep it down.

Jennifer stood next to Amy "Me either". She hissed as her hair came lose, and flew round her head like an angry red flame.

"Simple, we just get back in the limo, and ask the driver to take us into town." Megan had her sensible head on. But when she turned around she found that the car was long gone, and their suit cases were left piled up behind them.

Hannah had to try and convince them it was going to be alright. "It might be OK inside" she said, trying her best to sound positive. She really wasn't happy that things weren't going her way. This was supposed to be her plan, the first step in starting her new life. She pushed the front door hard, trying to relieve some of her annoyance, and just like that it swung open. She need only have given it a light tap, but she wasn't the half-hearted kind of girl.

Clapping her hands over her mouth she could hardly contain her newly found happiness. "Wow!" she cried out in total amazement. The entrance hall was massive. There was no way the run down building outside could have housed a hall this size. It was wall to ceiling golden coloured marble. To the left was a large staircase, the carpet was a lavish red colour. There were black chandeliers hanging from the ceiling. The windows from the inside were stained glass, and depicted events that Hannah had never seen before. She called out to the girls, and Amy was first in pulling both hers and Hannah's suitcases behind her.

Suddenly standing in front of Amy was a man, he held out a hand to her "Allow me to help you, Amy is it?" He had appeared as if from nowhere. She felt like she knew him from somewhere, then it came to her. He was the man from the email. Hannah stood gazing at him. It was also the same man that was in her dream, as she thought this he turned from Amy and winked at her. Her heart was a total fluttering, pounding mess. He is more beautiful in real life she thought, not even questioning the fact that she'd had a dream about him, before she had even really had a chance to meet him. All she could think was that it truly was a dream come true. She shook herself. She didn't do mindless gawping, although apparently now she did. She could usually keep her cool, and hold her own around attractive men. He was different, there was something about him. His eyes? Or the way his hair sparkled like it trapped all the stars from the night sky in it? Or his body? Sure, he was clothed now, but she was lucky enough to have a glimpse of what was hidden underneath. Even if it was just a dream. She sighed and felt herself blush. This wasn't like her at all. Something about the dream had changed her. For the better or worse though, she was yet to tell.

He spoke again cutting through Hannah's thoughts "I'll see that all your bags make it to your rooms. If you make your way to the dining hall, I'll join you shortly. As for Amy here, she looks like she could do with some rest. I'll see her to her room" He put one arm around Amy's waist and let her fall into him. He then lifted her up and carried her effortlessly up the stairs. Hannah felt more than a tiny hint of jealousy surge through her. Why was he taking Amy to her room, he should be taking me. She pushed the thought out of her mind and turned round to meet the others as they walked hesitantly through the front door. The looks on their faces a mix of shock and amazement.

Cautiously Jennifer stepped forward "What is this place?" She seemed suspicious. Like she really didn't trust what she was seeing.

Hannah threw her hands up in the air. "Who the fuck cares!? Let's go eat! I'm starving!" She had sensed Jennifer's suspicions and knew she had to convince her she would like it here. I mean what was there not to like? The place was like a palace. It was way beyond 5*s on any hotel rating charts. She wasn't sure how high she would rate it, but it was definitely way off the ratings scale. Looking around in awe, Hannah spotted a sign above a large wooden door at the far end of the hall. It clearly read dining hall. How on earth had she missed that? She was so hungry, and it was like the sign, (and the door) just appeared by magic. The smell of freshly cooked food swiftly flooded the hall, and the girls happily followed their noses into the dining hall.

Once they stepped inside the hall they were not disappointed. For there was a large banquet table, laid out with all their favourite foods. Fiery Mexican for Jennifer, a pasta salad and pizza for

Hannah. She liked to think she was being healthy with the salad, but for Hannah, it was all about the pizza. Megan had a soft spot for chicken wrapped in bacon, and sauté potatoes. She also loved curry, and it seemed to just appear in front of her. A large lasagne sat untouched on the table. Amy's favourite.

The Realm Of The Wolf

Amy woke up. She was cold, so cold. This wasn't the soft warm bed she was promised. Where had that mystery man taken her? Where was he now? She felt like he was close, watching her. She couldn't see him, but that didn't mean he wasn't there. She could hear a voice but couldn't tell if it was his or not. She couldn't tell what it was saying. She didn't want to know. Whatever it was, it couldn't be good. This place didn't feel good to her.

She could feel something. It was snowing. She was covered in snow. No wonder she was fucking freezing! She was wearing a summer dress in a blizzard. She tried to stand, the surface she was on was unstable. It rocked and creaked. She was sure that snow wasn't forecast, this just didn't make sense, but she couldn't have travelled that far, after all he only took her upstairs, didn't he? She couldn't be sure though. She felt like she had been to sleep and had woken up in a nightmare. All she knew was that she was so cold, and the surface she lay on felt ridiculously cold and hard, it was like it bit into her skin.

What she was on was a frozen lake. As all her senses slowly returned, she looked around and was able to take her surroundings in. Snow covered the land as far as her eyes could see. There were no trees though, no anything, just snow, and this lake she was on. She started to panic, there were no trees, and no oxygen. She couldn't breathe, she felt like she was suffocating. She wanted to scream but couldn't catch her breath to make a sound. What she didn't know was why there were no trees, no air. Where was this place? The answer she didn't get, to the question she couldn't ask, was that she was deep in the Realm of the Wolf. The Werewolf.

****

Hannah was sleepy and full of food. She left the others in the middle of the feast to retire to her room. Not that she knew where it was. When she stepped out of the dining room, she was back in the entrance hall. She had the overwhelming desire to head up stairs and so she did. After all she was sleepy, and it made sense that her room would be up there, somewhere. She felt annoyed again, why hadn't he taken her upstairs? Show her where her room was.

Once she was upstairs she was greeted by a long corridor. There were doors down each side. Lots of doors. Each door looked the same and none of the rooms were numbered either. Great, she thought, how am I meant to know which door is which? The more she stared down the corridor the longer it seemed to get.

There was nothing for it then, she would have to try each door one by one. She ran up and down trying each door. But none would open. She pushed with all of her weight against each off the doors. Where was that mystery man when you needed him? He would surely be able to help me find my room, Hannah's mind was starting to wonder. She couldn't shake the image of him from her mind. His beautiful black diamond eyes, his shiny black hair that looked like it contained the whole night sky. Long hair didn't normally do it for her, but she would make an exception for him. If only he hadn't of done a runner with Amy, that is. Then she heard a scream from behind one of the doors. Amy's scream. It brought her back to the moment. But Amy was with him. What was he doing to her? She pushed the horrible thought from her mind and followed the screaming to a door. Like all of the other doors she pushed and pushed against it. Then she noticed the handle and the plaque above it that said pull.

Feeling slightly stupid, Hannah pulled the door open. She felt bone chilling coldness against her skin. What she saw was white, bright blinding white, in fact all she saw was white. She stepped forward into the stark brilliant whiteness, she shivered all over. What she felt was a bitter biting coldness. She felt chilled to her very soul. Nowhere on Earth should ever be this cold, she thought to herself. Then she reminded herself, this truly wasn't anywhere on Earth, how could it be? She felt something else too, it didn't take her mind off the feeling that she was slowly freezing to death. If anything, it added to the discomfort of the situation. Whatever it was, she could feel it was wet against her skin. *Snow*? It was snowing. Once her eyes adjusted to the brightness she found she could see for miles; she was in a forest. Wearing her vest top and jeans it was no wonder she was freezing cold, and what's more, she was confused. How could she be in a forest? She was inside, she'd walked through a door on the first floor of the hotel, (or whatever it was,) how could she be outside? She looked all around. Looking finally down at the ground she saw foot prints. Amy's foot prints. No one else would wear heels in the forest! Hannah ran in the direction of the prints. She had to follow the footprints before the snow covered them. Before it hidden them all up. Before they were gone, not just now, but forever. Before Amy was lost. Forever. Hannah's mind was working overtime. She didn't want to think any more. Her mind racing, she knew what she had to do. Hannah ran. She had never ran like this before in her life. But then again she had never really needed to. This time she had a reason to. She had to save her friend. She had to save Amy.

Soon the forest was behind her. In front was only white. Ice cold whiteness. The soft crunchy ground beneath her feet was replaced by something else. Something that creaked, and rocked. It was slippery and unstable. Without realising it, Hannah had ran on to a frozen lake. She heard more screams. It was Amy. She wanted to run to her. She couldn't waste a second, her friend was in trouble. Fear rose in her, she couldn't think about what she would find. All she knew was that Amy needed her. Taking a deep breath she focused her mind on the task, and ignoring the loud groaning of the ice beneath her, she started to run again. No sooner had she started when she was stopped.

A wolf! And not just a normal wolf. No, that would have been bad enough. This was a fucking large wolf! It stopped her dead in her tracks. She tried to look past it but couldn't. Its eyes meet hers. Hannah wasn't tall by human standards. She was 5'4, however when a wolf meets your eyes at 5'4 that's a pretty damn big wolf. She blinked the snow out of her eyes. The wolf wasn't a thick set wolf. It was bony and looked emaciated. It looked starved almost to death. Hannah sized it up, it might be big, but it looked so weak, so pathetic. She felt a flush of courage pulse through her veins. I could take this wolf she told herself. Take it she did. She pushed its head to her left then kicked it in the side. It took all of the strength, but she did it. I'm not even sure how she managed to do it. The wolf went skidding off across the ice. Hannah wasn't going to let it get in her way, she was going to save her friend. She ran forward again, slipping on the lake.

She ran towards the screams. Now they sounded distant. They sounded like they were under the ice. Amy had somehow fallen through the ice. Someone else was on the lake with her. Hannah caught a glimpse of something, it was dark and seemed to beckon the snow around it, concealing its true shape, its true identity. Whatever it was it had Amy, and it was taking her with it through the ice. It was pulling her through the icy water and into another realm. But what was it that pulled her through? Hannah still couldn't be sure.

As you could probably guess, it was the vampire. It was taking Amy to a Realm where he felt more at home. Hannah felt helpless. She had no idea what to do. She certainly didn't know that when you access a realm from within the vampire's castle, where they were, the rules of the Under World were broken. Realms could cross over and interlink. Anything was possible. So Amy really could have gone anywhere. Wherever she was now the ice had re-frozen where she broke through. Which given the temperature of this place was not surprising. Hannah beat at it with both hands balled in to fists. She beat hard. The ice was harder. Much harder. She had to get through. Amy was down there somewhere, under all the frozen water. She had to be down there.

Something grabbed her ankle and pulled her away. She dug her nails in, like a cat hit by a car on the road. She turned to fight off what was dragging her away. She expected to see the wolf. Instead she saw a man. A naked man. She turned back to look into the lake, to the spot where she had last seen her friend. She heard one last scream, and it all turned red. The pure frozen white water was tainted in a flash with the warm rich red. Amy's red.

Hannah was now screaming. The ice of the lake was so cold it was burning her skin as she was dragged over it.

She put her hands round her mouth, like it would help somehow and called out "Amy!!!" she screamed it out with pure desperation.

The man spoke "It's no good, she's gone. She is in their realm now!"

"Their realm!??" Hannah asked back confused, and angry.

"Yeah, the vampires!" He snorted back "but hey, I have you" Hannah couldn't read his tone.

He stopped not far from the bank of the lake, and let go of Hannah. She tried to get up and run away. He jumped forward landing on her back, knocking her down hard back on to the surface of the lake. The force knocked what little air there was out of her lungs. More than that, it shook all of the bones in her body. *I should be broken, be dead. Maybe I am dead,* she thought. It would make sense. Maybe it's all a dream and I'll wake up, she told herself. Just like that dream in the limo, maybe I haven't woken up yet. She wasn't hopeful of that. The only thing she knew for certain was that, awake or dead, she was moving again. The cold icy surface of the lake was jagged and rough from a fresh fall of frozen snow, and ripped at her skin like chips of broken glass. He pulled her back all the way to the bank. When at last he finally got her there he slowly rolled her around until she was pinned underneath him. She could feel an intense sense of conflict coming from him. He was radiating uncertainty. Part of him wanted to bite her, and rip her apart limb by limb, and taste her flesh, and feel real blood run over his teeth, and inside him. It had been too long since he had feed on the human soul, he now wanted the human itself. The other part wanted to touch and feel the softness of her skin. To soak up the warmth of it, to kiss it. To kiss her, and make love to her, to something that felt real. He had enough of sucking the energy from empty feeling souls, he got no real satisfaction from them in any way shape or form. He could make love to her then kill her. The thought of it crossed his mind. But when he kissed her, and felt the passion and lust behind it, he didn't want to kill her. He wanted to keep her, to have her forever, over and over again. Hannah felt something too, the thing she had missed for so long. The feeling of being wanted, of being needed. She missed it, and now she had it she didn't want to give it up.

Even though the snow rained down endlessly on their naked bodies it didn't bother them. Nothing, it seemed, could stop them. Nothing, that was, until the other werewolves sensed her presence. They wanted a piece of this new energy force, this ball of power they could feel emitting itself from on or around the lake. It was like a beacon calling to them. Then one by one they let out a howl. Each more chilling, and deadly than the last. It wasn't a pack calling out to each other, it was a series of warnings. These wolves lived and hunted alone, and each one treated the other as a threat. There was no alpha male, no head of the pack here. As far as these wolves were concerned they were all alphas. Well, in their own heads they were. It was a hard time for the wolves, and the souls in their realm were slim pickings. It seemed no one had the fear of them that they used to. No one came to spend eternity being hunted here. There were new realms, new fears.

Now however there was a real chance to fill up and recharge

their energy, none of them were going to miss out on this opportunity. One by one they made their way down to the frozen lake. Their thin, emaciated bodies seemed in no way to do these true beasts of hell justice. Their hunger did however make them deadly.

Hannah suddenly felt the true coldness of the realm again. She looked up feeling slightly abandoned. Slightly hurt that it had all ended so abruptly. Then she heard the howls. Fear filled her every cell. She knew now she was in danger, real danger. The mystery man that stole away her friend didn't seem to scare her half as much as the howls of these monstrous hounds of the Under World.

She felt something hit her. It was her clothes. She didn't have time however to put them on. The first wolf had already made its way to the lake, and was running across it with an urgent speed Hannah could never hope to match. She didn't need to worry though. Her lone wolf was back and now he was fully powered up. He seemed to have bulked up, too. His skin was full and firm. Where there was once skin and bone there was now full on rippling muscles. She could see them flexing under his fur. She didn't understand how this had happened nor did she really care at that moment in time. All she cared about was getting to safety, and she knew this wolf would keep her safe.

She didn't know how she knew she was meant to get on his back she just did it. Just like riding a horse she told herself. Hannah hated horse riding, she went once for Megan's birthday. The others loved it, she did not however. It made her feel sick, and terrified. That was nothing compared to how she was feeling now. To top it all off she was naked, and being chased by staving wolves. They were now coming at them from all over the forest. A few times she felt a tooth or two graze her leg, she tried to blank out the short bursts of pain. Soon she would be safe, she would wake up and be at home in bed, safe. Except she didn't have a home or her own bed any more. She tried not to think of that either. The wolves were getting faster, but they could never quite catch them.

She tried to breathe and found for the first time that she couldn't. The trees had gone, it was all white again. Before this became too much of an issue her skin felt something cold and hard.

It wasn't snow, it was too hard. It was marble. She was back in the castle. She wasn't sure what had happened, had she fallen off the wolf? She couldn't be sure. Sure of that. Sure of anything. She had somehow managed to keep hold of her clothes, she wasn't aware she had even picked them up. Quickly she dressed. She looked around for a sign of the wolf, or the man. She was alone, really alone. Had any of that really happened, her mind was running on overtime trying to process what had happened, then her thoughts turned to Amy. Where was she now?

***

As Amy slowly opened her eyes she felt weak. Drained. Like she had just fallen through a sheet of glass, and been ripped open all over. She didn't know if she was alive, she didn't feel like she wanted to be alive. She wanted to be dead. For the first time in her life, she felt like she'd had enough. Opening her eyes, and trying to lift her head, she saw the realm of the vampire. Only for a second or so, she was the first human to witness the realm as a, well, human. As she cast her eyes over the gleaming white streets, and up at the buildings (made of what looked like a mixture of what she could only guess were human bones, and beautiful precious gem stones,) she whispered a prayer to herself. She was sure that it would never go answered in a place like this. *Let it be quick, let it be painless.*

After her time was up, (that's possibly the nicest way to put it) her soul departed from her body, and wondered off into the realm. Her soul was for a short time at least unaware that she had left her body behind. Then, when the realisation kicked in, and she looked back at all that was left of her once beautiful body, she ran off into the streets in no particular direction, as she ran she was screaming, and crying. Who could blame her for being hysterical, after everything that had just happened to her?

A vampire took her away under the pretence of having a 'good time'. He promised her so many things, to be his queen, to have whatever she wanted, whenever she wanted it. All she had to do was pick a door. Any door. After all there were plenty to choose from, the corridor was never ending, and lined with doors. Like a twisted genie he allowed her to make her wish before she pulled the door open. A wish that would never be granted. For he hadn't the skill or the care to make that wish come true. Empty worlds and lies were all he had for her. Well, that and the overwhelming desire to feast on her life force.

Amy was excited she was finally with a man that appreciated her.

She smiled and made her wish, she had experienced some strange things with men, and carried out some bizarre requests, and been dumped in some horrible ways. But she was sure this was going to be different. How wrong was she? She was expecting the world, so to speak, when she opened the door. What she wasn't expecting was to be dumped on to a frozen lake. Then to be picked up and thrown at it in order to crack the surface. If that wasn't bad enough, as the ice cracked underneath her she was dragged through it! While he dragged her through the ice, he bit her and drained all the blood from her body. Doesn't sound like much of a fun time to me.

The vampires circled the remains of her body. Poking her and prodding her. Wondering what this flesh and bone creature from beyond their realm really was. She was brought to them by their master, and left by him for them to finish off. He was done with her. He had other toys to play with.

"Step away from the girl" Snarled a voice.

"Who says that? And what authority do you have here?" Shouted one of the vampires, looking around in alarm for the culprit.

The voice snarled again "I said step away from her!" it was angrier this time.

"Her soul has departed now, and it walks amongst us," said a different, wiser female vampire.

"You have no authority here, dog!" Spat another.

The werewolf stepped forward, and changed into human form. Looking around, he saw the soul of Amy, lost and scared, wondering around amongst the vampires.

He wasn't in the mood to take shit from vampires, especially when they had something of his "Then her soul at least is mine! She came to my realm and…." He broke off as he felt a hand touch his shoulder, it forcefully pulled him back. It was the female vampire that spoke before. He followed her to a quiet alleyway, where she offered him her long coat to cover himself.

She looked around shiftily to make sure no one was listening "I fear this is all my fault" She spoke sounding worried, she also seemed like she was shivering. Not that it was cold in the city where the vampires lived. It was heated by the burning red sun that cast a warm pinkish red glow over the Realm. It was her nervous state of mind that caused her to shiver, she felt uneasy about the events that were unfolding all around her. Events that she had unwillingly set in motion.

He paced back and forth "And how is that so?" He answered questioning her logic.

She looked around again "I've been up there." She pointed up at the sky.

He took a while to think about what she was saying. "To the realm of the human? But up until now I believed that place was a myth." He wasn't certain that was what she meant, or if she was just crazy.

I was her turn to be annoyed now "Where then, did you think these souls that walk among us that we feed on come from? This aside, I've been there, I've seen it. I've lived with them. Been one of them. I kept a journal, talking about my feelings, experiences. About them, the humans. My father was snooping in my house and found it. I should have been more in tune with him then. He never takes interest in me. He asked questions, lots of them. So, feeling worried, I read his intentions. I saw in his mind, and saw what he was meaning to do. He went then to Lucifer, and planted the seed that he might be allowed to go there, where the humans live. After all, if the Almighty can send a creature from deepest hell to Earth, why can't Satan?" She shook her head, after seeing what her father had done to one human, and knowing what he was capable of. She hated to think what else he could do. Even full of hatred for the humans she had encountered, she would never wish her father upon the rest of them.

Still pacing and trying to process the information, he questioned her further. "But how has he done this?" he asked, still not sure that this woman wasn't just another crazed vampire that wasn't to be trusted.

She took a deep breath, shook her head in shame and continued "I overheard parts of their conversation. As his well mate, or whatever you call me, well me and Lucifer have a connection and I was able to get close enough to hear them, and anyway, Lucifer made some kind of porthole between here and Earth. Using his Palace, there is a room in there somewhere that he used his powers to make the gateway to up there. He also, I don't understand how, but he moved my father's castle to Earth. It used to be at the far end of the realm, over there in the mountains, now it's just mist over there as far as I can see. It must be to cover up the fact that the castle is missing. The thing is with my father's castle, well it's like a realm in itself. It is a world within this world. It's crazy, you can walk in one door then walk out the same door and be in a totally different place to where you were before." She wasn't even sure she was making sense any more, she just had to get it all out.

Feeling even more confused than ever, he rubbed his hand against his temple and looked up at the vampire "That could explain how he is able to get the humans in and out of my realm, there must be a link to it in his castle." He was trying to decode everything she had just said.

She still wasn't finished, she felt like she was making a confession and had to let it all out. "I think there are links to all the realms in his castle, he is the only one to have a castle like it, and the only one to be able to access the other realms well other than Lucifer that is." She looked away, almost ashamed. Until now at least she thought the vampire was the only one who could pass freely between the realms, {there may be one other who could also roam around freely, she didn't want to think about him right now though} and to top it all off here she was talking to a wolf. A creature that she believed to be a lower life form than herself. Nothing made sense to her any more.

Another voice now joined them in the alley way "Very good you two, very good" They turned around to find Lucifer standing behind them clapping his hands together.

He smiled at them both then continued "Well just think after tonight this will all be over, and he will be returned, and everything will be back to normal, and Aidan, you can go back to the dogs, and Adrianna, you can go back to being my bitch" He stepped in between the two of them.

They both took a step back away from Lucifer "You have a name too?" they said in unison.

He slapped them both on the backs and then he winked at them before he carried on talking. "Well ain't you the lucky ones? You both have names. He, on the other hand, has not. He was the first thing I made, and stupidly I put lots of my power into. When I realised what I had done, I also thought I needed a way to control him. So I invented the name rule. If you have a name, that makes you more powerful than something that doesn't. It's as simple as that really" He flashed them a smile.

Aidan stepped away from Lucifer again and turned to face him "So we are both more powerful than him?" He asked, sounding confused.

Lucifer put his palms together and looked at the ground, it was like he was praying. "In theory yes, you should be, but no one has ever taken him on, as fear also gives you power, and well, I didn't really think it all through properly, to be honest" Lucifer shook his head, and looked like he was deep in thought. He sounded distant, and concerned.

"So how will he get back?" Adrianna was intrigued to know.

He was still looking down, he couldn't face either of them now. "Through the porthole. The castle came out though the mouth of a cave, and will get sucked back through at midnight." Lucifer said half-heartedly.

Adrianna still wasn't done with the questions. "When's midnight? And what is it? It's not something I'm familiar with here," She paused and cast her mind back to her days as a human. She was sure that midnight happened on Earth, but in the Under World no one had any concept of time. Anyway she was sure that wasn't the important part. She still had more questions that needed answers. "And what happens if he gets out of the castle?" Adrianna was feeling even more worried about the situation.

Aidan was pacing again. He felt uneasy about the whole thing too, but still wasn't sure why he cared so much. Why did these humans mean so much to him? Did it mean he may have a chance to redeem himself for all the terrible things he had done? Why, all of a sudden, did he care for redemption? He pushed the questions away. They didn't really care for him anyway, and he was sure that whatever he was feeling, it was only because he wanted to feast on their souls.

Looking up at Lucifer, Aidan fixed his eyes on him, he was begging. "I'll make sure he doesn't escape, if you let me in to your castle. I'll keep an eye on him" He offered. He was really pleading more than offering.

Lucifer was unsure, he didn't know who to trust right now. "Hmmm, and what's in it for you?" Lucifer asked uncertain of why Aidan was so keen to help.

Not breaking eye contact with Lucifer he had to convince him he was sincere "I want to make sure the other human girl is safe" he was being honest.

Lucifer finally got his smile back. So the wolf did have a weakness he thought to himself. But now wasn't the time to exploit the wolf, he needed his help. Still smiling he wanted to see how far the wolf really was prepared to go. "Other girls you mean, there are another two you are yet to meet. But ok, I don't see why I can't let you help me. Ok I'll let you, just follow me." With that, Lucifer led Aidan away and they went to his castle. Adrianna was left alone, feeling useless. She would find a way to help yet though. She had to, it was her mess, her fault. There was no way she would just stand by and let her father escape. The world of humans was dangerous enough as it was. It didn't need vampires added to the mix. She couldn't bring herself to think of the destruction he could cause. The humans wouldn't stand a chance. They would all be doomed. There would have been a time when she would have welcomed that, but things had changed.

Rescue Me

Hannah was trying to feel positive, she needed a plan. A way to get help, to get out of this hell hole. After all, this was all her fault. She was the one that left Richard. She decided she needed a holiday. She picked this place, and convinced her friends it was a great idea to come here. Some great idea that turned out to be. However, now wasn't the time for pity, it was time for action. She would find Jennifer and Megan, and Amy wherever she was.

She would find her, Amy would be OK, and she tried to convince herself. They would all be OK. She pushed the image of the lake out of her head. The flash of red jumped into her mind. She forced it back. Amy was just taken that's all, she would get her back, would free them all from wherever they were, and she would get them home safe and sound. She knew that. She was Hannah, she always got her own way. She knew something else too, she wasn't alone. In the time that she had dressed, and sat and tried to work out her plan, she felt that she was being watched. Feeling brave she called out.

"Hello, I know you're there. Whoever you are, I'm not afraid, so show yourself!" I'm not afraid any more, was what she was thinking, but maybe now she was a little. She could sense something, like when you know someone is behind you even when you don't hear them creeping up on you. Something else happened then that caught her attention. Music. Music playing from the dining hall. Although the sign above the door now read DANCE HALL.

***

Jennifer could hear loud dance music. It stirred her from her sleep. She could feel it all around her. Buzzing through her veins. Her foot started tapping, and when she sat up she started nodding her head in time to the beat. She couldn't ignore it any longer, she had to dance. She didn't know the music, but to hell with it. She didn't care, it was calling to her inner dancing demon. Taking over her inhibitions. Once she started dancing she couldn't stop. Not until the music did. Even sometimes that wouldn't stop her from dancing. Now she felt sure she would never stop. Dressed in her best silk night dress she rose up from her bed and followed her heart. It was telling her to follow the music, as for her head it, was lost in a dream. She was in a club. She was a dancer in one of those cages on the side of the stage. She was good, everyone was watching her, and they loved it. She was loving it. There was so much love in the club, in the air. The music really made her feel in love. It was euphoric, and enchanting at the same time. She danced out through her bedroom door and in to the dance hall. The floor lit up, there were disco balls everywhere, and laser lights and smoke machines. A few strobe lights. In her head this was the best club ever.

***

Hannah had a feeling she knew she would find someone dancing away in the hall. She didn't have to second guess as she was right. It was Jennifer. Lost in a trance. Hannah looked up and saw beautiful candelabras with black glass, and painted ceilings depicting things that she had never seen before. Gods that looked like stars and the moon. Trees that turned into people, a woman that wore clothes made of grass. It was truly bizarre to her, but beautiful none the less.

Whatever music Jennifer was dancing to it wasn't the same music that Hannah was hearing. Hannah could hear eerier haunting music, to the likes of which she had never heard before. It was like Jennifer was sleepwalking, well sleep dancing, and Hannah couldn't find a way to wake her up. She was mesmerised by how she moved. She was so full of energy. It was like the music was fuelling her, making her dance more. The more she moved the more energy she had. She couldn't stop. Not now. Not ever. She didn't even notice Hannah, let alone that she was in the same room as her. She did however notice the door that appeared at the far end of the dance floor. She danced her way over to it, and as she got closer to the door, it opened. She danced through the door way and was gone. Hannah went to run over to the door but it was gone before she could get there.

It was then that Aidan made his presence known to her. He grabbed her by the arm and spun her round. She gasped when she saw him. He was the last person she expected to see.

"I don't have time to dance." She said urgently, "I need to get to Jennifer, now! I need to save her, I need to help her! Now!"

"I think I know where she is, we just need to find out how to get there" Aidan's words were just as desperate as Hannah's.

"We, wait, what's with the 'we'? I don't even know you. Not really, why do you want to help me?" She really was far too confused with the situation as a whole. She didn't need anything else to add to it. Especially not men.

"I think I am the only one that can help you, and you can't do it alone, it might be too late to save your last friend, but if we move now, we should be able to save this one" Aidan was concerned that Lucifer didn't really have the situation under complete control. The fact that he had let Aidan help out, and granted him permission to enter his castle did little to calm Aidan's feeling of unease.

"What do you mean, it might be too late to save Amy, what do you know? You must know something. Tell me, what, have you seen her? Do you know where she is?" Great, she had more questions, and was aware she was wasting more time. However there were things she had to understand.

"There's no time for all these questions now, we need to move, and fast. If he has taken her to where I think he has, we really don't have time to wait around discussing the what's and where's to do with the other one" Aidan was quickly losing his patience. Werewolves were notorious for having short tempers at the best of times due to their animalistic nature, and this situation really wasn't helping matters.

Hannah was upset, and angry at his lack of compassion "Her name is Amy!"

Aidan shrugged his shoulders "OK well, that's great, but are you coming with me or not?" he didn't care about her name, he didn't even really care if they found her, not really. Besides it wasn't in his nature to care. He just knew they couldn't stay put for long. It wasn't safe. Especially for Hannah.

His nonchalant attitude was really pissing Hannah off "What choice do I have?" Hannah couldn't lose hope, even if Aidan didn't care, she did.

Aidan had already started to walk off "None, if you want a chance of finding your friend alive." He shook his head, what had he gotten himself into? Well, he was in too deep now to just give up. He wasn't even sure he could, he was trapped within the vampires' palace now. A place that even Lucifer couldn't control. He could access it through his castle, but that's as much as he could do. He had given the vampire complete control of the palace. And it was the vampire that was setting all the rules. This was, as we know, no ordinary vampire. He was dark and twisted in ways you would never want to imagine, let alone experience.

Dancing In The Dark Side

Jennifer really was in a night club now. Deep in the realm of the vampires was the club it was called Semi-precious. All the dancers were named after semi-precious gem stones. All bar one. Jennifer. She was dancing on a platform next to the main stage. There were vampires everywhere. They couldn't take their eyes off of Jennifer. The way she moved, the way she smelt, the way she looked so alive. She suddenly came out of her trance. Feeling scared. She saw all the hungry eyes gazing up at her, and panicking she started looking for a way out.

A hand grabbed her from behind. She turned around and saw black eyes. Dark hair. Pale skin. She wanted to scream. He put his hand over her mouth, and shock his head. No one will save you. That's what he meant. She could sense it then that she was doomed. There really was no way out. He dragged her through a curtain at the back of the platform. It was like the curtain Hannah had crawled through in the limo. Like liquid, but dry. That's a contradiction, I know, but this whole place is one big contradiction.

On the other side of the curtain they were in a long dark corridor. It was poorly lit and had doors down either side. The walls were red, the doors painted black. Matte black. Glancing at them as she was pulled past, Jennifer could see scratch marks on the paintwork. How many girls had he dragged back here? It was best to not think of that now. She needed to think of a way out of this situation. She tried to desperately scratch help me as she was dragged on but it was no use. It was helpless. She was helpless. There was nothing. No one that could save her now. Why would they? What had she done to deserve any help?

Finally he stopped outside a door. The sign on it read PRIVATE. He kicked the door, and it burst open. Once it was dramatically opened he dragged her inside. The room it was dark, darker than black, if that's possible. A door sprung up in place of the one that was knocked off its hinges, it slammed closed and the once darkened room erupted into life. A chair appeared in the middle of the room. Drapes flowed down the walls. Candles burned in the corners of the room. Large black pillar candles. The flames didn't flicker or stir. The air was still. Jennifer took a deep breath. Was there any air? Was she even breathing? Did she even need to? It wasn't like she could ask. What would the point be? She was sure that even if she was breathing that she wouldn't be soon.

He took his place on the chair. Lifting his pale hand and gestured her towards him with his finger. She obeyed. She couldn't see the point in not. Having one last glance behind her. She wasn't surprised to see that the door had sprung up moments ago had now gone. There was no way out. Even if there was, where would see go? Her heart started beating faster all of a sudden. She was afraid. Knowing now she was truly facing death. He was beautiful. Not at all her normal type. But hey it wasn't like she could say no. She flicked her hair back and tucked some of it playfully behind her ear.

Music started playing. True to form Jennifer started dancing. Firstly on her own. Then she slunk over to him. She had given plenty of lap dances in her time. But she was determined to make her last one her best. She writhed around in time to the music. Letting his hands make their way all over her body. They stopped at the top of her thighs. He kept one hand there, and then moved one to her shoulder. He pushed her hair back and pulled down the strap of her night dress. He kissed her. On the shoulder. Then all the way up to her neck. His hand up moving up her thigh at the same time. She wasn't wearing any underwear. The same time as he realised this, he decided to sink his teeth into her neck. He tasted her blood. He was unsure about it to start with. But quickly got a taste for it. A taste for her. She was different to the other one. Her blood tasted more vibrant, more alive.

Jennifer writhed partly in pleasure, partly in pain. He body was confused. Her mind conflicted. Then something else started happening. A ripping pain stirred deep inside her. Her soul was being torn from her body. She really was dying. She was in so much pain now. It was pain the likes of which she had never experienced before. It was like she was being torn in half. Somehow, in a place deep within herself, this pain made her feel strong. She called upon her anger. Her inner strength. He would stop doing this to her, she would make him stop. No man, human or otherwise would inflict pain upon her. Not without her consent. She mustered together all her strength, both physical and mental and pulled herself away from him. She was seconds away from the end. From her end, and she lived. Well, was just about alive, for now at least.

Second Chance, No Choice

He was shocked. Truly shocked. This had never happened before. Sure souls had resisted him, tried to fight back. But they could never succeed, never match his strength. Not like this. Then he had an idea. Jennifer saw a sparkle in his eyes. Like a black diamond that just caught the light. His mind's cogs where turning in full motion. He liked this one. She showed promise. There was a fierce streak in her. She wasn't giving up without a fight. He needed someone like this on his side. In his realm. He needed to add a new dimension to things. To add new levels to his castle. He had vampires, plenty of them. He need a new type of vampire. A new fear to keep his realm going when he was gone. She was just the thing. But not like this. He had big plans for her.

He pushed Jennifer away from him and she fell onto the floor. Then slowly he offered her his hand. She took it begrudgingly. Try as she might she couldn't find the strength to stand. She was feeling incredibly weak, after she had exerted the last of her strength in her bid to get away from him. She was finding it too hard to keep her eyes focused, and her legs were shaking uncontrollably. Standing was definitely an issue. It all took far too much effort. She knew however that she needed to keep going. She needed to follow him, to wherever he would take her. This would be her life now. There was no hope of getting away. This time he led her from the room. He didn't drag or pull her. Was he showing her kindness? Surely not. No he was trying to keep her alive. He needed her alive.

He walked her slowly to the door. The door that wasn't there only moments ago. It felt to Jennifer that he was almost aware of her weakness, like he was showing her some kind of compassion. He could have killed her. But he didn't. All the time he was thinking, plotting. Then it came to him. The way she moved was mesmerising. He could have her as a dancer in his club. However he had plenty of them. No he had another idea for this one.

He had stolen a goblet from his master, a beautiful black glass goblet. Or at least he thought it was black glass. It had a beautiful gold tint to it, like sparkling gold veins that ran through it. Giving it a luminescent life. Not really like cold boring dead glass at all. Rumour had it that it was the glass, or goblet if you will, of eternal darkness. A glass that could give someone eternal life in the Under World. Now he had it he couldn't wait to try it out. To see if the rumours were true. If so he would be the first of his master's creations to create something himself. The created would become a creator. He liked this idea. He liked it very much.

He knew just the place now that he would take her. Turning the handle on the door he opened it slowly. Adding to the tension he paused before he opened the door. Turning around, he glanced at Jennifer's face and smiled, then he walked into the room, taking Jennifer in with him.

It was his bathing chambers. The one Hannah dreamt about. If only she had shared her dream with the others. Jennifer might then have felt slightly more afraid. As for now she felt nothing. Not fear, or excitement, or dread. She didn't even feel numb. Nothing could explain or describe her lack of feeling. Looking around the room, she didn't know then that she would have an eternity to study it, she tried to take it all in. It wasn't to her taste, it wasn't really her style, but was up to her standards. It was all a bit too black and gold for her.

When she had finished gazing around the room, her eyes fixed on the pool in the centre of it. He was already bathing in the rich warm red waters. Or at least so she thought it was water. Stupidly she was thinking that there really was no other option, she walked towards the pool. It looked so warm, rich and inviting. Just what she needed to relax her aching body. She hurt all over. Not surprising really considering the fact that she almost had her soul ripped out of her body.

Slowly she eased herself in, it was deeper than she had expected. The water came up to just below her chin. This made her feel uneasy, she didn't like deep water. She wasn't a great swimmer, preferring to laze around on the pool side in her bikini rather than do any actual swimming. Her nightdress wasn't helping the situation either. So she decided to ditch it and wiggled her way out of it. It dropped to the depths of the pool. Once free of her dress she thought she would give swimming a go. She didn't really have a choice, she couldn't touch the bottom of the pool.

The water was splashing in her face, getting into her eyes. It was thick. Thicker than water should be. Only too soon she began to realise as she cautiously made her way over to him, that this wasn't water. She tried not to think about it. It was difficult to start with and made her feel like gagging. It was getting into her mouth and she couldn't spit it out without more running in. She had to swallow it, and try not to choke on it. But it wasn't right, she shouldn't be drinking blood. She had found something that made her feel more uneasy than water. She never thought that would be possible. But then again swimming in a pool of blood could be quite an unsettling experience. Then she stopped thinking about it, she looked down at it and looked up at his eyes. They held her concentration. She was suddenly over all her fears, she wasn't afraid of water, or blood anymore and she found herself by his side in no time.

He hugged her, a gentle hug to start with. Then he pulled her in closer. He wanted to feel her heart beating. It was calm. This did surprise him somewhat, hugging her closer still he smiled. Soon she would belong to him forever. For a while he forgot the bigger picture that he planned to be surrounded by beating hearts forever. He was lost in the moment hypnotised by the sound of her heart. It would take him some time to get used to the sound. Souls were silent.

Too Lost In You

After making their way through the dining room doors Hannah and Aidan found themselves faced with a long hall way lined with doors. Yes, more doors. What can I say, this vampire just loves his doors. They frantically tried every door, some they even tried more than once, but it was no use. They were all locked shut. Not one of them would open. Push or pull it made no difference, they wouldn't budge. The main doors, to the dance/dining hall had vanished.

"It's no use, I'll be stuck in here forever!" Hannah cried. Aidan tried to comfort her, he put his arm round her. He had seen some of the scared souls do this to each other, and assumed it's what they did when they were afraid. Afraid of him.

"I'm not used to having to comfort things, I, um, but I'll offer what I know of comfort to you now" Even his words seemed awkward.

Hannah smiled, for a brief moment she felt something. She felt safe.

"Why can't the men where I come from be more like you?" She asked more to herself than to Aidan.

"See now you're being more positive, talking about men where you come from." He was trying hard to put a positive spin on things. This was all so new to him.

"But don't you see I'm never going to be able to get back to them, and I don't want to. Not to the men at least." Hannah felt like finally she could let her guard down, she felt like Aidan wouldn't judge her, or try to change her. He wasn't Richard.

Aidan pulled her in tighter, "If only he would let me keep you" he whispered more to himself than to her.

"Wait? What did you just say?" Hannah felt something different now. Anger. "Keep me? Keep me! I'm not a possession. Just when I was starting to think you were different it turns out your just the same!" She pushed him away. She didn't want him near her.

"Sorry it's been ages since I've had a mate, and I'm not used to it, and…" Aidan tried hard to resolve this totally alien situation.

"A mate! In whatever term you mean that, I don't like it, Ahhhhhhh! Fucking men!" She hit the door in front of her with her fist. It hurt. But it didn't hurt as much as her feelings. What Aidan had said really struck a nerve. Even if she didn't want to admit it to herself at the time.

"Look I'm not like the men where you come from, I'm not a man to start with, and I'm not human, so you can't compare me to one!" To prove his point he phased into a wolf. This time he wasn't the strong wolf that Hannah remembered. He was thinner, smaller, and weaker looking. When he phased back in to his human form it seemed to take ages, and to Hannah it looked really painful too. When he finally turned back in to Aidan he looked hollow, not full of life like he did before.

"You look thinner or something?" Hannah wasn't really sure what to say.

"It's because I haven't fed in a while. I need to hunt. I need to feed. You've distracted me for too long, now I'm weak, I'm no good to you or myself." he turned to walk away, it was no good, he needed souls, he needed energy to feed on. This human, she would bring him to his end, he was sure of that. She wasn't good for him, he really wasn't good for her.

"Wait you're not leaving me, how do you, um feed? What do you eat? Do you know a way out?" Again Hannah was full of questions. Always questions, never answers.

Aidan paused, he didn't know a way out, that much was true, and why hunt when he was sure Hannah could provide more than enough energy for him? Why ask her permission? Why need it? He really did feel like he was going soft. *No wonder no one was afraid of werewolves any more,* he thought bitterly to himself. There was a time when they were more feared than vampires, now they were nothing. Reduced to hunting for scraps of souls who had wondered unwittingly into their realm. If he was to live up to his reputation as fierce and unjust as he was in his former glory days, he was going to take what he wanted from her, regardless of whether she liked it or not. He leaned forward and kissed her. She was still angry and tried to push him away again. She felt sure that in his weakened state she would be stronger. She was wrong. Even now he could overpower her. How had she managed to stop him before on the lake? That seemed like forever ago. She tried not to think about the lake, and lost herself in the kiss. She liked a strong passionate man. After Richard she needed it.

After what seemed like an eternity of pleasure, Hannah felt alert. Her head was buzzing. Aidan felt stronger, more alive than ever. They were ready to take on anything. The only trouble was the castle still seemed to be against them. It was almost like the castle was trying to protect its master. They went from having loads of locked doors to no doors at all. Looking around they appeared to be in a golden marble cell. No windows, or bars. Just wall to ceiling marble.

"Oh my god, we really are fucked! Where is it we need to be? Where did you say you think Jennifer could be?" Hannah was freaking out. She hated enclosed spaces.

"I didn't, and I don't think it matters now. We really are trapped!" Now Aidan was angry.

"There has to be a way out of here, there just has to be!" Hannah was starting to panic even more

"You should never have let me discover you, you shouldn't even be here, now you are, and everything is messed up. I'm trapped in some idiot vampires hell tower. I shouldn't even be in this realm. I don't belong here. I should have stayed with the wolves. I should have left you! And I should never have trusted Lucifer! He said I could help him. He is just fucking with us, all of us!" Aidan would have more than a few choice words to say to Lucifer when he next saw him. If he ever saw him again that was.

"Left me? Left me to what? To die? I wish you had. Then I wouldn't be stuck here now."

They were both angry now. But getting angry was making everything worse. The anger was feeding the room. Like a living breathing creature that fed on hate. Was it hate that kept the vampire's home running? Hate that fuelled the palace that bent and moved to the vampires every whim and wish? The more they shouted at each other, the smaller the room got. It took them awhile to realise this. It wasn't until they realised they couldn't step back to get away from each other, and that they were being forced together that they noticed. They went silent. Both together. Staring at each other. The room wasn't working against them, they were both to stubborn to realise it was pushing them together.

The White Light Chronicles: The Red Cliffs

Hannah held Aidan close. She felt like she was safe. If only for a while. There was still so much about him she wanted to know. He carried so much pain inside him. She wondered, *had he ever had any one special in his life? Sure he had a mate, but someone that really meant something to him.* That had to be different? The question began to burn inside her, so she took a deep breath, and asked, fully prepared for an angry response.

"So has there ever been a special someone or, um, something in your life?" There was a long and awkward silence. Followed by a growl of annoyance from Aidan. He hated feeling this way, this vulnerable. Plus now wasn't really the time for a heart to heart. However he decided to answer. He knew she wouldn't give him a break if he didn't.

"Hmm, well there was someone once, a long time ago. A shape shifter that went by the name Caterina. In her human form she looked like your average lonely woman. She lived in a small house not so far from here. She had lots of manky looking, I mean horrible, hideous cats as pets. It seems that people were afraid of crazy cat ladies. Like I said, were. When she transformed into her cat-human form she was amazing. Not that it matters now" He paused and sighed shaking his head he continued "It turned out people weren't that afraid of her for very long, and when Lucifer decided he no longer needed her, he took her away. He personally raped her and tortured her, until she begged for him to end her." Aidan felt furious now all his memories of Caterina came rushing back into his mind. He thought hard to push them back.

Hannah was curious, if he ended her, how did he do it? She thought better than to ask though. There were more important things to worry about now. Like saving her friends. Although something else played on her mind. It had been playing on her mind for a while. Like those eyes. Both sets of eyes. Were they watching her now? Was that how they controlled what she could see, and where she was? The thought made her feel sick. Extra eyes inside her head spying on her. It was such a massive invasion of privacy. She blinked and thought she saw them. Who's eyes where they? The vampires were black? Well dark, deep and dark. But Lucifer's, what where his like. Was it really him she saw in her dream?

"What does he look like, Lucifer I mean?" She was now more curious than ever to know.

Aidan paused. "Hmm um tall, skin head, lots of muscles, and weird markings on his skin, why do you ask?"

"Oh no reason" Hannah smiled. This wasn't how she saw him at all. Which struck her as odd. *Maybe it wasn't him, then.* She told herself. Well, you and I know both know it was. He looks different to each and every one of us. But Hannah didn't know that at the time.

"I think she will be in the club" Aidan decided to take charge of the situation. Too much time has been wasted talking about things that didn't matter right now.

"Oh, well that's helpful" Hannah replied, sounding very sarcastic. Luckily for her werewolves didn't get sarcasm.

"That's, OK, hmmm, that's odd" Aidan's hand was groping at the wall behind him. "I think I can feel something, feels like a door handle." He was unsure but suddenly felt calmer.

"Seriously? You're not joking with me?" Hannah was trying hard not to get her hopes up.

"I didn't really mean what I said, you know about wishing I'd left you to die, I was just angry. I just thought I should tell you this now. Before I open the door. I mean neither of us know what's on the other side, this could end badly for both of us, and, well, I wouldn't want it to end with bad feelings between us and…." Not that he truly understood what it meant to have good feelings, or any real feelings at all. This was all still new to him.

"It's OK," Hannah cut in. "You don't need to explain yourself or apologise to me." She was really eager for him to open the door. She wanted to save her friends, and every word he said was holding her up. There simply wasn't time for this right now.

Finally, Aidan opened the door.

No Help For The Helpless

They walked, or rather stumbled into Semi-Precious. The club was buzzing. All the vampires were talking about the latest snacks to enter their realm. The special treats that their master had bough to them. It really was true, there really were humans. Adrianna wasn't crazy after all. Flesh and blood beings that walked around in a land far above them. It was all true. They were much tastier, and satisfying than the souls they fed on. If only they could feast on blood all the time. If only they could taste the energy of a living soul all the time. How much stronger they would be. They would be able to establish themselves as the most feared creatures in the Under World for sure then.

Aidan instinctively put his arms round Hannah. He knew he had to protect her as much as he possibly could. It wouldn't take long before the vampires realised that they were there. Then things certainly would go badly for the both of them. There was no way Aidan could take on all these vampires. Even full of energy like he was now. Many of them were also full of human blood, and flesh. They had walked in to what felt like yet another trap.

He listened to the many conversations going on. To him it was like there wasn't any music playing. He could block it out and listen to any conversation in the club. It was one of the few perks to being a werewolf. All Hannah could hear was noise.

"There was one here." Hissed one vampire.

"Where?" snarled another.

"On the stage." Hissed the first vampire.

"Really, oh how exciting." Fake yawned another, unenthusiastically.

"Well, she has gone now." Snarled the second vampire.

"Gone where?" Asked another quizzical vampire.

"He took her!" Hissed the first vampire a little annoyingly, clearly they were fed up with all the pointless questions.

"Oh really? Well He would!" Added another very annoyed, maybe even jealous vampire. Not that vampires have much in the way of patience. Remember what Obsidian was like?

Aidan pulled Hannah closer, and said in her ear. "She was here."

"What? How do you know for sure? Wait so where is she now?" She turned to face him.

"He has her!" Aidan balled his hands into fists.

"He, who?" Hannah could see his muscles rippling under his loose clothing.

"It's hopeless. He is the most powerful vampire ever made, and Lucifer's left hand man so to speak." He spat out the worlds, full of rage and disappointment. Not a good combination for a werewolf to be feeling. He had forgotten what Lucifer had told him earlier about the vampire not having a name.

"Oh, shit. Well, that's not good. What do we do?" Hannah was trying not to sound too worried. Deep down, well not that deep down, she was scared. She could feel her fear levels rising. Her friend was with the most powerful vampire ever, and she was with a werewolf in a club full of vampires, with no obvious way out. Yes, the door they'd entered in had gone. Once again she finally figured out they were trapped, this definitely topped the shrinking marble cell though. In there they would have just been crushed. Here she would be eaten alive! She shuddered, trying not to think about it. She had something she needed to do. Save her friend. All her friends.

"I've seen where he took her" A voice whispered in Aidan's ear.

"Who's there? Who said that?" He replied, his heart would have been racing if he had one. He wasn't used to things creeping up on him.

"So many questions, why, there are lots of people here, and any one of them could have said it." The voice spoke again.

"But not all of them are hiding in the shadows!" Aidan didn't like playing games. He liked things on his terms. He was a king after all. Well, in his realm he was. It's just that none of the wolves respected him anymore. Not since all the souls dried up, and they all started to turn on each other. He was the only wolf with a name. He was, and still is the original werewolf.

"Well that's big, coming from you! Dog! You don't belong here anymore than I do. But then I don't belong anywhere down here. There are realms for vampires, for werewolves. For witches, goblins, trolls, devils with pitch forks. For dragons of sorts, and all manner of other creatures of the deep. But none for me. For the one this whole Under World shit tip was made for. No I have to hide, to move from place to place. I do so by using His castle. It saves time and effort on the walking front you see. So I know how this place works." His voice still a whisper. It was hard for Aidan to gage his tone.

"So you're the original one? The one cast down from high above? Then, it's true we can cross over?" Aidan asked feeling hopeful.

"No one from here is permitted to enter the precious land of the Almighty One. So forget it. Nothing you do will ever make you good enough to go there. You're a creature of the darkness, and so here you must stay" His tone was bitter, but there was a hint of pride mixed in with the bitterness. Like he had achieved something so few others had. Not that a massive fall from grace was much to be proud of. However without him, the Under World would not exist. Maybe he did have some reason to feel proud after all. And bitter.

"Why are you telling me this? Are you really going to help?" Aidan was once again getting angry.

"There is no help for the helpless, the girl will be dead I can tell you that much. I thought I was wicked, and cruel. But none can compare to Him. Not even the great Lucifer himself, and he knows it. Now if you wish to continue on this pointless mission, there is a door at the back of that stage. He took her through there. That is if the door is still there. Then you'll have to find the next door that he took her through. Know that and go fast, and you might just save her." With that he was gone.

Hannah was so overwhelmed by the club that she didn't even notice that Aidan was having a conversation. This was starting to feel like the best club she had ever been in. Aidan could sense it, sense that she was losing all her fear that she was starting to fall under the vampires spell. The club was just like a nightclub on earth. A really amazing club. It had the lasers, and light shows. The floor lit up and vibrated in time to the music. Hannah thought the whole place was amazing. Aidan knew he had to get her out of there, and fast. It wouldn't be long before the vampires noticed their presence. But how was he going to get her to the stage? He looked up. The dancing vampires were still in their cages, that was a good sign. They hadn't noticed she was there. Then he spotted someone. Magenta. She was a deadly vampire, the mate of the very vampire that was taking Hannah's friends, and she did not look happy. She looked like she wanted to kill. To kill all of them. She didn't like this new game he was playing. She liked his new plaything even less. It meant that he spent even less time with her.

Aidan picked up Hannah and threw her over his shoulder. This was sure to get a little attention, and a few vampires did look. Thankfully none of them noticed that Hannah was human. It wasn't until Aidan had carried her half way across the dance floor that they started to realise it. Magenta let out a shriek, and all the vampires looked at her. She smelt the dog, and the human.

"There are intruders in here! And you all know what we do with them!" She called out. This was one human she was determined that she would have for herself.

"Kill them, and feast on their souls!" Was the reply from some of the vampires.

"No, fools! Kill the soulless dog! But the human, She is mine!" Her voice echoed throughout the club, and the other vampires cowered, and bowed down to their Queen. At least they still respected her, even if her mate, their King did not.

Aidan picked up his pace, and started running. Hannah who up until now hadn't put up much of a fight was starting to get annoyed. She didn't like being carried, and now Aidan was running she was starting to feel sick. She was kind of missing the point. Aidan was carrying her to protect her from a bigger problem. He was getting closer to the stage, but the vampires were turning on him. Trying to stop him, trying to pull Hannah off of him.

The dancing vampires had stopped, and were swooping down from their cages. Aidan was hitting them back. Hannah had also redirected her annoyance to the vampires. It was a much better idea than beating up someone who was trying to help her. With all her strength she began beating them back as best as she could. They were outnumbered, and Aidan was sure they would never make it. A few vampires had bit him, and had drawn out some of his energy. Hannah had been bitten a few times to. Both weakened, they finally reached the stage. When they got there Magenta stood waiting.

"Did you seriously think you would be able to escape from here? I mean, I couldn't let that happen, let a human slip past me like that... And as for you, tut tut tut. Aidan, I thought you would have more sense than to come here again. Or is that it, are you trapped and you think that helping the human will help you earn your way out of here? Well, no such luck, as now you will both d…..″ She didn't get to finish her last words. Instead she lit up like she was filled with a thousand fairy lights. A thousand red fairy lights. The other vampires shrieked and cried out in fear. They had never witnessed the ending of one of their own before.

"She is full of energy and will burn for a while before she will finally perish, and then she will be lost forever. Shame, for she really was very beautiful, in her own twisted way." The voice whispered to Aidan from behind the illuminated vampire. It was the same voice as he had heard before. He had so many questions for it this time. The main one being how did he really end up down here? There was however no time to answer the question. The door behind the stage appeared, and it was wide open. Without hesitation Aidan, who still carrying Hannah, made his way through it.

The Cup of Eternal Darkness

Jennifer was suddenly aware she hadn't spoken in a long time. However nor had this creature she was with. She didn't mind though, looking into his eyes told her everything she needed to know. As for her voice, she felt like she had forgotten how to use it. She had forgotten everything else. Like her friends, her family, her life outside this place. She had given up on it all. Now looking up into these dark eyes, was she going to give it up for them? Looking deep into them made her give up what tiny dot of hope she had. He seemed to speak inside her head. *It's no use, you can't escape.* He smiled again. That same, pained expression. Smiling clearly did not come naturally to him. Jennifer tried to stir up a feeling of compassion, of caring. Nothing. She was full of fear now, and longing. Longing for freedom.

His expression changed then all in an instant. To one of real pain. He let out a cry, full of pain and anger, and vengeance. Jennifer felt confused, nothing in the room could have caused him pain. Then finally he spoke.

"You will pay for this with your life! Whoever you are, I will find you and end you!" The pain, and terror in his voice would make anything's blood run ice cold.

Now Jennifer was truly terrified. She wanted to say something but still no words could come to her.

"My poor, poor Magenta" He wasn't crying but it was clear he felt something deep down inside. Jennifer realised then that someone close to him had died, and somehow he felt it. He was linked to her, and would now be linked to Jennifer. She would offer herself as a replacement, if that's all she could do. Maybe this was how she would save herself. She didn't know that he had already made plans to keep her anyway.

"I might be a small consolation prize, but you can have me, for all I'm worth. I may not be much, but I can be anything you truly desire." She still hadn't lost it. Her ability to say exactly what men wanted to hear. She stroked his chest and gazed into his eyes. He soon seemed to forget about his loss, and the pain he was feeling.

His thoughts then turned back to the cup. He ran through all his thoughts about what the cup could do. But returned to his original idea. All he needed to do was put his energy, his life force into the cup, allow her to drink from it, and before she drinks the last drop say what he wishes her to become. It all sounded so simple, a little too simple.

First step, getting his life force into the cup. He lifted his wrist to his mouth and bit down hard. However not even his own teeth could pierce his skin. He was getting angry again, Jennifer could feel the way he tensed up in her arms. Trying to comfort him she lifted her hand, gently she ran her fingers through his hair. After he felt more soothed she turned her attention to the cup. It was made of what looked like black glass, with a mysterious gold tinge to it, that only showed in certain light. It had a thin delicate stem, and the glass its self was a simple design. Nothing fancy, no ornate swirls or etching. He turned the glass around in his hand, rubbing the stem between his thumb and forefinger. It rotated round and round. It was then that Jennifer saw it. A single red gem stone. How could he have missed it?

She reached out to touch it, and the second she made contact with it a blade shot out of the stem. It cut her wrist. Instinctively she knew she had to put her own blood into the cup. No sooner did she do this that a black blade came out of the other side. This blade was sharp and pierced the vampire's skin. He smiled an almost happy looking smile. A glowing red, well it wasn't really liquid it was almost like a stream of glittering red lights poured out of him. He allowed it to fill the cup before he healed himself.

Then he passed the cup to Jennifer, who was still bleeding. She took it and stared to drink. As she drank he began to mutter something chanting louder and louder. He was saying

"A mermaid deadly, beautiful, and unfair. With flaming long blood red hair. With piercing eyes, and sharpened teeth. She will lurk in the waters deep beneath. When souls into the water bathe, they go to their final grave. She will come forth to have her feast. My beautiful, deadly beast."

At first nothing happened. Jennifer felt the same. The vampire seemed very disappointed. Then something did happen. To start with it felt like pins and needles. A slight painful tingling in her legs, it however slowly got worse. The bones in her legs began to snap and brake, the skin on them ripped and twisted. She wanted to scream, to cry out for help but the pain was too great. The bones started to regroup, to reform, and her skin knitted itself around them. Her torn muscles took on a new form. Once it was over she looked down, it was difficult to see much through the blood pool they were bathing in. She went to wriggle her toes backwards and forward. She couldn't.

She no longer had legs, she had a tail, a fish like tail. But it wasn't scaled like a fish, it was skin. Her skin. She was like a dolphin. She felt sick, what had she done to herself? She couldn't control her new tail, it was alien to her. It was also painful to move. It ached in ways her legs did not. She then caught sight of her hair in a mirror, it was now a vivid blood red colour, and her eyes were red too. Then running her tongue over her teeth she felt that they were all razor sharp. Like a sharks. She really, truly had become a monster. She wanted to cry, but couldn't find the tears.

He had done it. Created a new creature. Now he had other business to attend to. Time, for now, was very much not on his Side. As much as he wanted to test out his creation. He had more Important things to do. He had to carry out his plan.

Jennifer was feeling frustrated the vampire left her. She was now alone, trying hard to get to grips with her tail. But she couldn't master it, she couldn't get the right motion. It was tiring, and it hurt like hell. She was now too annoyed and exhausted to cry. She was out of breath, even though she no longer needed to breath. She was a creature of the Under World now. However old habits die hard. To top it all off, she was stranded in the middle of the pool. She couldn't really swim when she was human, let alone now she was like this. Out of energy, and hope she started sinking. She was drowning and didn't even care. Jennifer was dying. In her heart she was already dead, the old Jennifer was well and truly dead, and the new her might as well die to. Taking in deep breaths she let the liquid fill her lungs, there was no fighting it, there was no fight in her. She heard drowning was quite euphoric. She was willing to try anything. She still knew how to breathe, still had her lungs.

Her soul was still resisting the urge to leave her, even though her body was giving up. Her soul knew what was out there, and it was safer where it was. In her new body no one would feast off of it. With that it mind it decided to take control. Flowing through her, it energised her, like electricity running through her veins. It gave her new life, and animated her. With one rush of energy she forced herself to the surface. Gasping, as if for air, she finally made her choice, she wasn't going to give up, and anyway why should she? She had been given a second chance, and was alive. Well, at least to a point she knew she was living. She knew something else, too. She was hungry, and someone was coming. The footsteps were close. Hiding now just below the surface, she blended in perfectly, moving from side to side, the pool stirred. It was the only indication that something might be lurking in the depths. The footsteps were getting closer still.

***

The pool as you know it's filled with blood, and as you also know nothing in Hell has blood in it. The creatures don't nor do the souls. So I hear you asking how does the vampire have a pool full of it? And why doesn't he just drink it?

Well, the answer to the first question is that the pool is filled with the blood of those on Earth that take their own lives. Lucifer has his minions out making collections from all the dead bodies buried above the Under World. Up until recently, he kept it in his own castle. However like most things, he gave it to the vampire. It was a bargaining tool, you can have the humans and your own pool of blood. It was Lucifer's way to keep the vampire in The Under World. But to answer the second question, the blood of the long dead goes stale quickly, and tastes bitter. As soon as the vampire tasted the fresh rich blood from humans, it just confirmed what he wanted. Live humans, warm blood. Not this pool full of death, and dead blood.

Destination Lost

When they burst through the door they weren't in a corridor. They weren't even in the castle. Aidan felt uneasy. They were in a forest. But not his forest. It was dark, and misty. The trees were old, ash, oaks, beech. The thick trunks were close together, and the air was heavy. Hannah was feeling trapped, she was scared and wanted to get out of the forest. Aidan could sense this, but he didn't know where to go. Since Caterina had died he had no more reason to leave his realm. He wasn't familiar with all the new realms, or with their locations. He found the realm of the vampires, no problem, he could feel their energy and power. He had no idea who or what lived here. Nor did he really want to find out. Hannah could taste something in the air, it was stale, and made her feel sick.

"What lives here then? Hannah asked trying to sound calm and breezy.

"If you want my honest answer, I don't know. I've not heard of a realm like this before. It could be new. It does happen. New fears make new realms" Aidan knew he probably hadn't helped to reassure Hannah, but he could pretend.

"New? But it feels old!" Hannah was more confused than ever.

"Well there were no trees in hell until recently. Until you and your friends turned up, with your need for air no doubt. The whole place seems to bend to accommodate you." Adrianna had talked about humans needing air. Word gets round I guess.

"No air? That's odd, so the trees in your, um realm, is it? They weren't there before? So this forest is all created so I can have air, well me and my friends. My friends! Oh my god I forgot, well not forgot. What if one of them is here in this forest. Megan always found woods, and forests scary. She hated Snow White, oh you wouldn't know what that is, unless there is a fairy tale realm or something. Maybe Megan is here!" Hannah was getting excited now. She wanted to save one friend at least. Megan had done a lot for her recently, and what better way to return the favour than to save her soul?

"Finished talking? OK good. I think I saw something moving in between the trees" Aidan was peering out into the forest, moving his head this way and that, trying hard to catch a glimpse of whatever it was he saw.

"Oh wow!" Hannah put her hands over her mouth like an excited child trying to hold in a scream. Then she pointed. "Look! Look I see it, well some of it!"

A black unicorn walked out from between the trees. Its horn, eyes, and hooves glowed red. Steam came out of its nose and mouth. Aidan and Hannah looked at each other, of all the things they were expecting this was not it. Its hair seemed to glimmer and almost move, like it was alive. They were mesmerised by it. Then they heard a noise they both knew, an owl hooted. The unicorn had a look of terror in its eyes. It shot of back into the forest. The owl hooted over and over again. Then the forest came to life. Little red lights lit up all over the place. Like berry lights on a Christmas tree. Hannah smiled. It looked beautiful. She had forgotten where she was. Nothing was beautiful in this place. Not for long anyway.

Aidan felt a chill creep over his skin. A black unicorn was the symbol of death. It meant that someone in this realm was going to die, forever. They would have no soul to leave behind, so they would truly be ended. He saw one when Caterina died. He knew now where he was. He was in the realm of the Black Unicorn. Close to the valley of true death, and very near to the realm of the fairy tale. Not that he knew that realm was there. He might not have visited all the other realms but he knew where some of them were. He thought he could find Caterina and save her. He couldn't. But as for Megan, was she even in the fairy tale realm?

Is Megan's Time up?

Megan woke up, she was still sat at the dining table. Everyone else had gone, she hadn't remember going to sleep. She didn't know the others had left her, she didn't know what was happening to them either. Which was probably for the best, considering what they were going through. What did she know? Well, she did know she was uncomfortable, she also knew that she was cold, and still very tired. She needed her bed. Or any bed, for that matter, would have been nice at that time. Slowly, she got out of the chair. The table had been cleared, which was odd. Why did no one wake her? Oh well, they must have decided to go to bed and leave her there, sounded about right.

She slowly made her way across the room, she ached all over. Sleeping in a chair is never a good idea. When she got to the doors of the dining room, she pushed them with all her weight, they wouldn't open. She tried pulling them, still nothing. There was, however, another door.

Megan looked at the door, something told her not to go through it. Something else told her she needed to get out of the room she was in. She tried the main door one final time. It opened. Now what to do? She looked at the new door, shook her head and walked through the main door. *Stick to what you know,* she told herself. But this place didn't exactly give you what you would expect. As for Megan, she wasn't where she expected to be when she pushed the door open. She was in a reception area. But not the large marble hall of the hotel. It was dark, and there was no one around. The only thing that lit up was a light strip on the floor, like the kind you get on aeroplanes.

To the right she could see a sign that read 'Gift Shop'. When her eyes had fully adjusted to the dim light, she realised that the gift shop was walled off. She could see into the gift shop. The wall was glass. She could see her reflection, she looked pale, too pale. "I need to get a tan booked when I get home, this is not a good look" she shook her head in disbelief at her appearance. She then looked for a door into the gift shop. There was none. The only way to get to it would be to follow the light strip, and walk all the way around whatever this place was. She didn't like that idea one bit, it made her think of her first trip to Ikea, she hated the fact that once she was in there she couldn't get out until she had walked through the whole shop and warehouse. She knew one thing for sure now, she certainly wasn't in Ikea, and she was starting to wish she was.

Taking a deep breath inwards it was time to be brave. There really was no going back now. She walked forward, following the way lit by the strip. To start with it was just a corridor, nothing scary about that right? Then she heard a whole load of bizarre animal like noises. It was like she was in a zoo. Megan didn't like zoos. It upset her to see all the animals shut up in tiny cells when they should be roaming free in the wild. This zoo seemed different to the ones she was forced to go to as a child. The corridor opened out into a large hexagonal room. Along the walls there were doors. *Hmm, what is it with this place and doors?* Thought Megan. Above each door there was a sign, one read 'Birds of prey', another 'Cute but deadly'. Others said thing like 'Night time dwellers', and 'Under the sea'.

She didn't like the sound of under the sea, and didn't trust this place one bit. She knew that by going through that door she truly would be at the bottom of the sea. She was also afraid of the dark, and didn't want to face that fear either. She didn't want to face any of them. With that in mind, she sat down on the grey carpet and looked up at the grey walls. She could happily sit there forever. Not having to go into any of the rooms. That would suit her just fine. However after, a while of just sitting she started to feel anxious. Like she was being watched. She turned around to find that the door to one of the rooms behind her had opened.

Water had started trickling towards her. Then it flowed faster and faster. Before she knew it the water was up to her ankles, and rising quickly. Then something started banging urgently against the door frame. It was trying to get out. Cracks appeared above the door, and all around its edges. It seemed like whatever it was, it was winning the battle against the door frame. It was going to give way. Megan was trying not to panic, but the water was rising. There was no way out. No safe way at least. Feeling scared and doomed, there was nothing for it, she ran to the closest door. It was hard to open it as the water filling the room was putting up resistance. So with nothing to lose she pushed it. The door swung inwards taking her with it. Quickly she shut the door behind her. Some of the water had gushed in after her, but not as much as she had expected. Then the water started creeping backwards, and out of the room. It slipped slowly under the door, like it was afraid.

"Great, even the water doesn't want to be in here." She had a really uneasy feeling about the room now.

It suddenly went dark. Beyond pitch black. Megan tried to let her eyes adjust, but they couldn't. There was not even a hint of light to assist them. Then out of nowhere the music started, jungle sounds, animal calls, birds taking flight, all over a drum beat. It was very atmospheric. Almost like a real zoo. Slowly the room got lighter. Megan noticed she could smell things, animals, she guessed. The smells weren't unpleasant, quite the opposite in fact. When it was finally bright enough to see, she realised she was in a large room, there were glass walls to either side of her, filled with exotic looking plants, and there was a path laid out in front of her, it looked like wood chippings, and smelled like it to. The place was set out like a maze, only Megan didn't know that just yet.

She walked up to the first glass cage, it seemed empty. Well, she didn't think it had any animals in it. There was nothing in it. Apart from the lights, hundreds, no more than that, thousands of tiny lights lit it up. Then she realised that they were hanging off of beautiful flowers, and their stems. How had she not seen the flowers before? The lights were illuminating the cage with a pulsing, colour changing light. It seemed to beat in time with music. It was amazing. Megan had never seen anything so magical in all her life. Slowly she slipped into a trance, hypnotised by the lights. Then when she was under their spell, thousands of tiny Under World fairies, with sharp teeth, and red eyes swarmed forward, angrily attacking the glass. Pounding it with tiny fists, scratching, and clawing at in with their razor sharp nails. But the glass didn't give way, of show any sign of damage. She breathed a sigh of relief then stepped back, the shock had brought her out of her trance. She was sure that the other cage was further away, now she was almost pressed against it. She was also sure she felt a tapping on her shoulder. Slowly she turned around.

Above this glass cage there was a sign, it read Graeae. Inside, there were two old, withered looking ladies. They looked like hags, like how Megan would picture them from the fairy stories her mother would read her. With hooked noses, and long matted grey hair. Although these had no eyes, they hand long spindly fingers, which fluttered almost like eyelashes. It was after studying the hands that Megan noticed their eyes. They were in the palms of their hands. Megan felt nauseous. Things like that turned her stomach. She looked away when she felt something sliver past her leg.

Walking forward she realised that the path branched off, and she could go either left, right, or straight on. She felt it again. This time it slivered between her legs. She shivered. It felt like a snake. She didn't mind snakes that much, it was spiders she really hated. But she would take them over the things in this place. Bearing her fear of snakes in mind, she should be truly terrified of what she saw next. However, the sight of an Echidna, half snake with brown, green and black scales, and half beautiful woman, with long shimmering blonde hair and big dark blue eyes. She was more mesmerising than scary. She felt like she could watch her for hours, slivering from side to side behind the glass. It was almost like she was trying to hypnotise Megan, but it didn't seem to be working. Failing that she launched herself at the glass, but hit it with such force she knocked herself out. Megan tried not to laugh, it was the first funny thing she had seen in a long time.

Something warm on the back of her neck soon made her see sense again. She could smell burning! And the whole place was getting hotter by the second. She glanced down one of the paths and saw fire. Something was heating up the glass it was trapped behind, she could hear it beating at the glass, then heating it again. "Good old Chimaera" hissed the Echidna she was conscious again. "We knew he would come through for us in the end."

Megan wanted to talk, to say something but the sound of glass smashing stopped her. The thing had escaped and from the heat of its fire she could tell it was getting closer. She wanted to run but didn't know which way to go.

She could see it coming into sight, she it through the flames. It was stopping in front of a cage, with his huge lions head it was breathing fire against the glass. The creature inside was banging on the glass. Then, smash! Another creature was free. Then smash, another. Frozen by fear Megan willed her legs to move, and when they did she ran faster than she had in her life. She could hear lots of hell's worst creatures being unleashed from their cells and they were behind her, chasing after her. She didn't look back to see what they were. She ran this way and that through the maze of cages. Some broken, others not. Some creatures had turned on the others and eaten them, the place was strewn with carcasses. The sight of them made Megan heave. But on she ran. Until she saw a door. She had never been so happy to see a door in her life.

Great, she was back in the grey room. The water was up to her waist, and rising fast. The creature that was trying to escape was still beating against the door frame. All the other doors had vanished. She felt like Alice trapped in some warped Wonderland. But she didn't have any magic potion to take. Big or small, there was no way out, no safe way. She was down the rabbit hole and further. Down in the pits of something seriously evil.

The water was up by her shoulders but that was the least of her worries. There was a loud bang! The creature had broken through the door. Tentacles wrapped around her legs, she tried to struggle free. It was no use. This creature was not going to let her go. It had a head like a crocodile! That's the last thing she thought as it opened its enormous mouth. It lifted her up by the ankle and tossed her into its monstrous jaws.

She waited for the agonising pain of teeth crunching down on her.

Nothing. She was on a slide! Whizzing down so quickly she was sure she left her stomach in the creature's mouth. It was dark. No lights anywhere. Down she slid faster and faster. Then, just like that, it stopped. She had stopped. The floor felt rough, and hard, not like the soft cushioned play mat at a park. But then she wasn't at a park.

Megan slowly got to her feet. She felt sick, and dizzy. She wasn't sure what was going to happen next. She didn't want to know. She wanted it to be over. This was worse than any nightmare she had ever had. Then she saw flashing lights in the dark. And a sign. 'WAY OUT'!

It was a way out but out to where? The sign above 'WAY OUT' read 'Rest Room'. She had nothing to lose and felt like she needed a little rest after all the running, and falling. She pushed the door open and found herself in a large golden marble room. There were candles flickering and burning in the corners, and dark red drapes on the walls. In the centre of the room was a large round pool, sunk into the floor. The water although red looked warm and inviting. Megan felt like a nice soak in a hot pool was exactly what she needed right now. She stripped down to her lacy purple underwear, she didn't know who else might end up joining her here, so didn't want to risk being caught totally naked, and lowered herself into the pool. The water was warm, but thick. She tasted a tiny bit then spat it back out. It tasted like blood.

Something was stirring in the pool, Megan realised now just how much of a stupid idea this was and tried to lift herself out. It had hold of her ankle, and was pulling her down. She tried to fight it off but it was stronger than her. It was pulling her under, she caught a glimpse of it. She saw red hair, and flame red eyes. It looked evil, it looked crazy. Then it bit her, it bit her all over. Megan tried to fight it off, however it had gone in to a full on feeding frenzy. *She had survived all of those other creatures,* she told herself, *and she could survive this.* She was wrong.

Megan got weaker with the more blood it took. Finally, when she gave up hope, she experienced the most painful thing in her whole life. It was tearing her soul out of her body. She wanted to scream but her lungs were so full of blood she couldn't. She was drowning. She was dying. Then it all stopped. She was lifeless, soulless, she was dead. It was finally game over for another player.

Friends Reunited

Jennifer had made her first kill. Had fed for the first time in her new body, in her new way. She wasn't sure about the taste much, but the rush she got from it was amazing. Like nothing she had ever felt before. She had never felt so powerful, so in control. She could definitely get used to this new way, or so she thought.

She glanced down at the weak pathetic human in her arms. She couldn't believe that she was once like this. Now look at her. She took a second look at the limp cold body. Something about it, its long brown hair, the shape of its face. The eyes, hazel eyes full of fear. It seemed familiar to her. She turned it over in her arms. On the lower part of its back was a small swirly black tattoo. She recognised this too. She knew this person? In her old life. A life she lived not long ago, yet now seemed like an eternity away. It hadn't even sunk in that she was holding a human, not a humans' soul. Something else was on her mind.

Running though her head she tried to access her memorises from before she was like this. She knew they were there. Just below the surface of the new ones. She ran back through recent events. Being turned, being afraid. Having a meal in a creepy castle with... With? Why couldn't she remember? Who was she with? She knew she wasn't alone. There were people there with her. Her friends. Slowly it was coming back to her. She knew this person as she was her friend! Looking at the body again, she pictured it full of life. It was her friend! It was, it hit her then. It was Megan!

She felt sick. How could she have done this? What had she become? She was a monster! She had killed one of her best friends. Now she would have to live with the guilt forever. For now she would have to hide the body. She couldn't deal with it. She swam down to the bottom of the pool with Megan still in her arms. However she could hear something, something that called on all her senses. Footsteps getting closer. She could feel something else too, her hunger was coming back.

Fantasies and Fairytails

The unicorn had gone, but Aidan didn't feel reassured. He knew there would be more, and bigger more deadly ones as well, if the stories about this place were to be believed. But where to go? He had lost all sense of direction. It was like the whole realm had spun around him, and stopped, and now north was east and east was, well he had no idea. There were no sign posts here, no maps that showed the way. If you left your realm you were at the mercy of the Under World, and this place had no mercy.

"I think we should get moving!" Aidan tried to assert some authority over Hannah. She was, however, not listening. She had seen another door. Aidan, it seemed, had forgotten that they were still inside the vampire's castle. Although they could access all the realms through the castle, the castle still controlled when and where they went, and while he was still in the Under World, the vampire still controlled the castle.

She grabbed Aidan's arm and pulled him reluctantly to the door, Aidan didn't trust what he might find on the other side. However, more black unicorns were amassing in the forest. So he had little choice, he couldn't take them all on, and the penalty to kill a black unicorn was the same as if you were killed by one. You would be ended, dead, gone forever. So really, if he thought about it, his only option was to go through the door. Yet still he hovered by the door unsure of what to do. It took all of Hannah's strength to pull him through to the other side.

Everything smelt deliciously like roses, and yummy Turkish delight. The whole place seemed to sparkle, and glow, there were rainbows, and gingerbread houses. To Hannah this place was like a dream, no, it was better than a dream. It was real. Aidan, on the other hand, knew all too well that rainbows meant evil leprechauns, and the gingerbread houses were full of beyond wicked witches. This place was once the realm of the witches, but over time people developed new fears thanks to fairytales. Fears of going to sleep and never waking up, fears of never finding their true love. So the witches asked Lucifer if, rather than creating a new realm they simply recreate theirs. After all, witches do feature heavily in most fairy tales. Lucifer, feeling lazy agreed, and so the witches set out to reinvent their realm. As for where the fears came from in the first place? There is a demon in the deep that comes up with them. A little pet that Lucifer himself created. It comes up with thoughts and ideas that would terrify humans, and implants them into our minds. Like I said before, if enough people find the ideas scary, a new fear, and therefore a new realm, is created.

It was hard for Hannah to believe anything evil could be living in such a beautiful place. Aidan was in despair as he realised Hannah had learnt nothing in her time here. Nothing in this place was to be trusted. Nothing was as it seemed. If it was too god to be true, then it was. Everything you saw was all part of some creatures trick to lure you in, and torture you. This was hell after all, and not some fun playground. Aidan was aware that the witches could turn into princesses, and damsels in distress. However with loves first kiss, you were in for a nasty surprise. He kept a watch for anything trying to lure Hannah in.

It was crying, whatever it was, and Hannah knew she had to find it and help it. She couldn't tell Aidan, he wouldn't understand. How could he? So when his back was turned she snuck off to see if she could find out what it was. It didn't take her long before she found the source of the crying. A tiny fairy was sat on a pink mushroom sobbing.

Hannah gazed down on the fairy, making her 'oh my god that's so cute' face. "Hello, what's the matter?" She asked sounding genuinely concerned.

Looking away, hiding its face the fairy spoke "The evil witch tried to turn me into a mouse!" Sobbed the fairy, flicking round its mouse like tail.

Feeling really sorry for the little thing Hannah almost wanted to cry. "Oh no! Is there anything I can do to help you?" Hannah had to do something, she had failed her friends, she was not about to fail this poor helpless fairy.

The little fairy looked up at Hannah, full of newly found hope. " The cure is in the witch's house, but if I go in there the witch's cat will eat me. I would fly but I can't any more, she made me too heavy to fly!" The fairy sounded genuine enough to Hannah.

She was coming up with a plan of action, and making her way to the house when someone grabbed her arm.

"What the hell do you think you're doing?" asked a very angry Aidan.

She pointed at the fairy and tried to assert some authority over Aidan "Going to help that poor fairy, after some evil witch tried to turn her into a mouse" Hannah was attempting to sound brave and Important, like she was on a mission to save the world. The truth was she didn't even know what she was looking for. What if she got the wrong potion, and made the fairy worse? Or killed her? What if the witch turned up? She couldn't answer any of these questions, she didn't know how. All she did know was once again she felt useless. She couldn't really help the fairy, she couldn't help anyone. She didn't even know how to save herself. It was hopeless. She really was hopeless.

When she was about to give up the fairy whimpered. "It's a purple liquid in a pretty pink bottle, on the witches table!" It covered its face with its hands and looked away from Hannah almost ashamed of its self, or possibly its situation.

Aidan really wasn't happy now. "We can't go in there it's a trap, the witch will trap us and kill us, and then it really will all be over!"

He snapped at Hannah.

Hannah was convinced that she had to go through the door, no matter if it was a trap or not. She had nothing to lose. So what if she did die? She had nothing worth living for now anyway. It's not like she could just leave this place and go back to her old life. She had no life to go back to. No, this was it. She was going to go through that door no matter what.

It was just then, when she had made her mind up that Aidan shouted, "Get in the house, the witches are coming."

True to his word the witches were flying in thick and fast, casting spells and chanting evil incantations. The sky lit up like a firework display, Hannah would have thought it was beautiful, if it wasn't trying to kill her. Aidan pulled open the door and ground to a halt, Hannah rushed in after him. They were back in the castle.

There was a large pool in the middle of a gold marble floor. Hannah had been here before in her dream, she felt like she knew this place very well. Something was different this time. Something stirred in the pool. Hannah watched the ripples move across the pools surface. Aidan sniffed the air, then took in a few deep breaths. Not taking in air but smells. Scents that lingered in the room. He looked at Hannah confused, how could she not know? How could she not sense it? Oh yeah, she was human, that would explain it. He could see her now his eyes had adjusted, just below the surface circling around and around, watching with her evil red eyes, she was flicking around her flame red hair. Behind all the evil that had now embedded itself in her soul, Aidan could still tell it was Jennifer.

She looked right at him now, he gazed deep into her eyes, and saw the true horror of what she had done, of what she had become. That was it, then, all of Hannah's friends had perished in one way or another, and now if Hannah stayed here she would be next. She was already feeling the allure of the pool, wanting to bathe in it. Aidan couldn't let this happen, neither could Jennifer. She knew she was calling out to Hannah, sending out signals that were calling her into the water, 'well, blood', she couldn't help it. However she couldn't do it, she couldn't kill another one of her best friends. She wouldn't. Deep down inside her a small part of her humanity still remained. While it did, she would use it to save her last friend. She motioned with her head to Aidan, who looked at Hannah. She was making her way to the pool. He rushed over to her and pulled her back, almost knocking her to the floor.

"She must never know, any of this" Jennifer said, implanting the words straight into Aidan's head. He heard and understood, he could tell how bad Hannah felt about letting her friends down, and it would finish her off if she knew what had truly become of them. Then Jennifer said something else to Aidan. This time it was a warning.

"He is coming, he is close! My re-creator, the master of this place you must go now!"

Aidan heard the warning loud and clear, and taking a confused looking Hannah with him, he headed to the closest door.

The Blood Red Cliffs

Aidan halted. Hannah was just behind him, and hit him like a brick wall. They were almost outside the castle now. Hannah was almost free. He could see the real world. Could he see Earth? Hannah stepped past Aidan, and she could see it now too. What was the point now in any of it? She could just walk out and be free. But she could never escape everything that she had been thought this night. What was the point in walking out without her friends? Without Aidan? She had been through so much with him. She now didn't want to be without him. Then she heard them. The screams of her friends.

It was so loud she couldn't escape from it. "Help us! Save us!" They cried out in unison. Her friends, they still needed her.

They were close now, so close. Aidan knew he could never stop her, from falling into the trap. She ran straight out of the castle.

She felt something grab onto her but when she turned round it had disappeared far away into the shadows. Was it Aidan? She wasn't sure, but she didn't think he could move that quick. Or even leave the castle. It didn't matter, she was at the cliffs edge now. She would have to climb down. Climb down to join her friends.

Hannah had never climbed anything in her life, except maybe a flight of stairs. Now she was going to clamber down a cliff face to meet her friends. She could still hear them calling to her. So there was nothing else to do.

She eased herself over the edge. Her feet felt around for a foot hold. The cliff felt damp and slippery. She found what she thought was a tree root and rested her foot on it. Slowly, and cautiously she made her way down the gnarled cliff face. The tree roots were dripping wet, and slimy tendrils hung from some of them. It took her a while to make her way down. Finally her feet felt the sand of the beach. She stepped back to look at the cliff face. It wasn't tree roots she could see, but bones. Thousands of bones twisted and woven together, to form the grotesque cliff face. As for what hung from the bones, well it was flesh, and the whole cliff wept with blood.

The White Light Chronicles: The Red Cliffs

Hannah turned her face to the cave, feeling sick at the thought of what she had just clawed her way down. She could see the shape of it, like a vampires' mouth, wide open ready to bite. Sharp teeth ready to taste the flesh of the dammed. She was standing at the gateway to hell. Just inside she could see her friends, Jennifer, Megan and Amy. Just as she remembered them, and not as they were now, dead, disembodied, and demonized. They were waving goodbye to her, and fading away.

On the cliff top the old building was fading until it turned into a small star. It rushed over the cliff and into the cave. The mouth of the cave started to close. Hannah stood still partly sickened, and now partly shocked. The reality of what had happened was starting to sink in. She couldn't just stand there, watching helplessly as her friends faded away, and the cave mouth closed, cutting her off from them. From Aidan. From her new life, her new destiny. She ran forward. Into her future. Into the unknown.

Welcome To the Gates of Hell

It was dark, and hot. The walls were red with blood, dripping over the bones of the dammed, heated from the fires fuelled by their condemned flesh. Glowing and flickering like a hearts' last beat. There was no light at the end of this tunnel. Only eerie cries, and calls from the beyond. She walked into the back of a long queue of lost souls. None of them looked at her, or even seemed to notice she was there. One by one the queue got smaller, each soul would let out agonising screams as it was their turn to be judged. Like the queue of animals at a slaughter house, each soul near the front felt uneasy as they witnessed their fate.

One soul from the front now, Hannah saw what fate would become of her, a deadly beautiful vampire stepped forward to feast on the soul, wrenching something out of it, that would leave it cowering in fear as it would step up to a door and await its true fate. The vampire would then disappear, only to appear moments later. She would flash a wicked smile, open the door and allow the soul a moment before she would push them through. Through the door of white hot flames.

When she saw Hannah, she froze. Fear flooded every feature on her face. Hannah was human! Not a dead soul, but a human, from Earth.

"It is true, then, and worse than I thought. You are here, and human, that means he must be free!"

The story continues in book 3

Adrianna Blue: like My Heart

R J Truman

Made in the USA
Charleston, SC
25 June 2014